KOALA
BEACH
OUTBREAK

Books by Robert Elmer

ADVENTURES DOWN UNDER

#1 / *Escape to Murray River*
#2 / *Captive at Kangaroo Springs*
#3 / *Rescue at Boomerang Bend*
#4 / *Dingo Creek Challenge*
#5 / *Race to Wallaby Bay*
#6 / *Firestorm at Kookaburra Station*
#7 / *Koala Beach Outbreak*
#8 / *Panic at Emu Flat*

THE YOUNG UNDERGROUND

#1 / *A Way Through the Sea*
#2 / *Beyond the River*
#3 / *Into the Flames*
#4 / *Far From the Storm*
#5 / *Chasing the Wind*
#6 / *A Light in the Castle*
#7 / *Follow the Star*
#8 / *Touch the Sky*

KOALA
BEACH
OUTBREAK

BETHANY HOUSE PUBLISHERS
MINNEAPOLIS, MINNESOTA 55438

J
ELM

Published by Bethany House Publishers
A Ministry of Bethany Fellowship International
11400 Hampshire Avenue South
Minneapolis, Minnesota 55438
www.bethanyhouse.com

Printed in the United States of America by
Bethany Press International, Minneapolis, Minnesota 55438

Library of Congress Cataloging-in-Publication Data

Elmer, Robert.
    Koala Beach outbreak / by Robert Elmer.
       p.   cm. — (Adventures down under ; 7)
    SUMMARY: When thirteen-year-old Patrick and his family befriend a young Chinese immigrant who arrives in Australia in 1855, they face the prejudices of local miners.
    ISBN 0–7642–2105–1
    [1. Immigrants Fiction. 2. Chinese—Australia Fiction. 3. Australia Fiction. 4. Prejudices Fiction.] I. Title. II. Series: Elmer, Robert. Adventures down under ; 7.
PZ7.E4794 Ko   1999
[Fic]—dc21
                                          99–6414
                                           CIP

To

Nancy, John, and Aaron—

family builders.

MEET ROBERT ELMER

ROBERT ELMER is the author of THE YOUNG UNDERGROUND series, as well as many magazine and newspaper articles. He lives with his wife, Ronda, and their three children, Kai, Danica, and Stefan (and their dog, Freckles), in a Washington State farming community just a bike ride away from the Canadian border.

CONTENTS

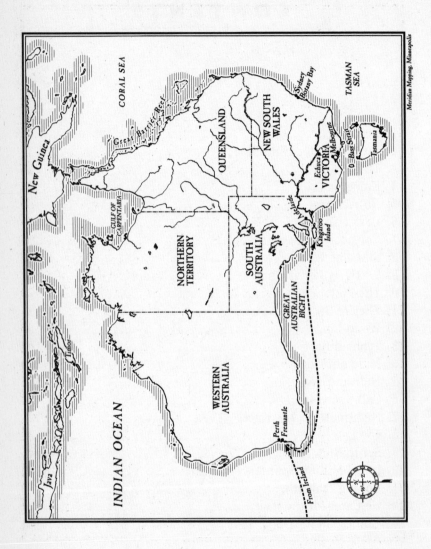

New Guinea

CORAL SEA

Great Barrier Reef

QUEENSLAND

NEW SOUTH WALES

Sydney
Botany Bay

TASMAN SEA

0 Bass Strait

Tasmania

Echuca
VICTORIA
Melbourne

GULF OF CARPENTARIA

NORTHERN TERRITORY

SOUTH AUSTRALIA

Adelaide

Kangaroo Island

INDIAN OCEAN

Java

Timor

WESTERN AUSTRALIA

GREAT AUSTRALIAN BIGHT

Perth
Fremantle

From Ireland

Meridian Mapping, Minneapolis

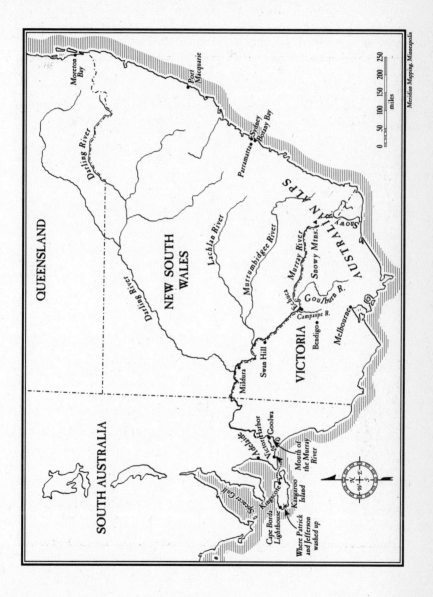

QUEENSLAND

NEW SOUTH WALES

Darling River

Darling River

Moreton Bay

Port Macquarie

Parramatta • Sydney
Botany Bay

Lachlan River

Murrumbidgee River

Murray River

AUSTRALIAN ALPS

Snowy Mtns.

Snowy R.

Echuca

Goulburn R.

Campaspe R.

Bendigo • Melbourne

VICTORIA

Swan Hill

Mildura

SOUTH AUSTRALIA

Spencer Gulf

Gulf St. Vincent

Adelaide

Victor Harbor

Goolwa

Mouth of
the Murray
River

Kangaroo
Island

Kingscote

Cape Borda
Lighthouse

Where Patrick
and Jefferson
washed up

miles
0   50   100   150   200   250

N
W • E
S

Meridian Mapping, Minneapolis

CHAPTER 1

SHIPWRECK

"Wait for us, Firestorm!"

Thirteen-year-old Patrick McWaid ran as fast as he could through the low, sandy dunes toward the salty sting of ocean air, but each step only filled his worn-out boots with more and more sand. Whose idea had it been to get out and stretch their legs?

Probably mine, he remembered as he tried to catch up with the others. While they had been waiting in line to load their paddle steamer at the river harbor of Goolwa, Patrick had suggested it was the perfect time to get off the boat and explore. And the ocean was only about a mile and a half away—an easy early-afternoon hike.

Finally he stopped, mopped his thick red hair back off his forehead, and watched the family's dog dart over a dune, yapping wildly. Firestorm was a mixed shepherd breed, only much smaller and with mottled reddish brown and gray fur. Patrick especially liked his dog's spunky ways and his strange eyes—one sky-blue and one brown.

"Don't worry, Patrick." Their American friend Jefferson Pitney led the hike through the low, rolling hills, kicking up sand and making big, round footprints. He was followed closely by Patrick's older sister, Becky, and their nine-year-old brother, Michael.

"That dog knows his way anywhere," Jefferson continued.

"When he gets tired of chasing sea gulls by an' by, he'll come on back."

"Hope you're right, Jeff." Patrick shaded his eyes and squinted as the wind whipped more sand into his freckled face. He wasn't small and round like his little brother, mostly just all-around average looking. Average, that is, except for the tide of freckles that flowed across his cheeks and nose, and the ears that always poked out of the side of his head until they were sunburned as red as his hair. Now at the end of the summer, they were most definitely sunburned.

"Of course he's right." Michael was convinced Jefferson could never be wrong. If Jefferson had promised Firestorm would come right back, then he would come.

"I suppose he *could* probably find us," admitted Patrick as they trudged on toward the ocean, somewhere over the rolling dunes. "Even if we sailed all the way back home to Dublin."

"Only that's not home anymore," piped up Michael. "The *Lady Elisabeth* is home, right here on the Murray River. Right, Jeff?"

"Sure enough." Jefferson raised an eyebrow, and the edge of his mouth turned up in a half grin.

"Home—it's just an expression," replied Patrick. "You know what I mean."

Patrick meant it. The river *was* home now. True, it had been harder for Patrick to leave Ireland than it had been for Michael. Their father had been unjustly accused of a crime and sent on the last prison ship to Australia. What could the family do but follow? So Patrick, Becky, Michael, and Ma had arrived in Australia a year ago, in 1868.

But the journey halfway across the world had been hard for Becky, too. Just by being a big sister, she had helped Ma keep the family together before they found their father. Patrick knew she had done a pretty good job of it, too. Most of the time.

She is *a lot like Ma*, he had to admit. Rebecca Elisabeth McWaid was petite and pretty, with a head of nut-brown hair and large, sparkling eyes that reflected the sun. Just like Ma. And when she hummed old Irish songs, everybody stopped to listen—especially Jefferson.

Michael, on the other hand, was a kite ready to fly away in the stiffening March wind. Round faced and sort of elf-like, he had questions about everything. And he was usually rescuing some kind of orphaned animal. So everyone had thought it was funny that Patrick—not Michael—had been the one to find their new dog two months ago in the river port of Wentworth. They had named the odd mutt Firestorm, a name that was only natural for a dog that had survived a terrible fire.

"Maybe all the birds leave for the winter," suggested Michael. They had just stepped out of the shelter of a low hill, and the wind grabbed the words right out of his mouth. It was March, after all, the start of Australia's cooler season. It wouldn't get as cold as a winter in Ireland, of course, but they were ready for sweater weather after the hot summer.

"What's that?" Jefferson raised his voice and leaned into the wind. He held on to Patrick's shoulder for a moment to keep from tipping over, and Patrick shouted into Jefferson's ear.

"He said, the birds are all hiding!" Patrick looked ahead to the beach, and it looked as if Michael was right. A couple of gulls raced by, tumbling in a sudden gust of wind. Becky gripped her skirt and squinted when a blast of sand hit her in the face.

"We should turn back," she suggested.

Michael shook his head. "We can't leave Firestorm here."

They paused for a minute, ducking down out of the sand that swirled around their heads.

"Once we make it to the beach," Jefferson finally decided, "we'll be out of the worst. It's not far."

Patrick nodded and blinked back the tears in his eyes. He tried turning around and walking backward. It worked for a few minutes until he tumbled over the crest of another sand dune and rolled down to the beach below.

"Here we are!" he shouted back at the others. The sound of his voice was swallowed in the crashing of waves. "Jeff? Becky? We made it! We made it to the ocean!"

But no one appeared at the top of the last dune. Jefferson and Becky must have fallen behind by a few strides.

"They'll be here in a minute," Patrick told himself as he dusted off his pants and braced himself to face the attack of the sea wind. It carried the full scent of the ocean, a heavy, alive kind of aroma, which tickled Patrick's nostrils. He smiled as he filled his lungs. The beach!

Out on the sparkling blue waves, a small ship fluttered like a butterfly with a broken wing, closer to shore than it should have been. Patrick could just make out its twin white sails and some of the people scurrying about on deck.

Closer in, a long line of fearsome waves rolled grandly into shore, only to dash themselves to death with thunderous foaming explosions. A furious wind carved the crowns of the waves into spray, flinging it into the sides of three or four cottage-sized rocks.

Turning his head to hear better, Patrick thought he caught a faint sound of barking in the distance. Maybe from behind the rocks. Firestorm!

"This is a good slide, Patrick," cried Michael. He giggled as he rolled over the top of the last hill to join his brother. "You should try it."

"What happened to Jeff and Becky?" Patrick asked.

"They'll be here. They were right behind me." Michael turned around to climb the hill once more.

For the next few minutes Michael played in the sand while Patrick scanned up and down the long, wide beach for any tracks that would lead them to his dog.

Where is he? Patrick could find nothing. But what he saw out in the water beyond the line of white-topped breakers made his heart stop.

It can't be! At first Patrick tried to convince himself that the ship was just turning around, heading back out to sea. It definitely seemed too close to the beach. But there was no doubt what was happening when a sail dipped into the waves and the two-masted schooner plowed its nose deep into a wave. As Patrick watched, the ship shuddered and broke into pieces on a rock out in the water.

Even above the whistle of the wind, Patrick could hear the sickening crunch of wood and the awful cries as men poured over the side and splashed into the water.

"Michael!" Patrick grabbed his brother's arm. "Run back to the *Lady Elisabeth* and get help!"

Michael did as he was told, scrambling for a foothold in the loose sand. He slammed into Jefferson and Becky at the top of the hill but kept running.

"Hurry!" Patrick yelled after him. "Bring back anyone you can find. We'll—"

"Oh!" Becky slipped down to the beach and stood staring at the disaster. She held her cheeks in her hands. "What can we do?"

"I know what *I'm* going to do," answered Patrick, unlacing his boots and pulling off his shirt.

"Oh no, you don't. It's too dangerous." Jefferson followed Becky down to the beach and put his hand on Patrick's shoulder. Patrick tried to shrug him off.

"I'm going!" insisted Patrick.

But Jefferson only held on tighter and shook his head.

"You're not going out there, Patrick. It's too far. You don't need to prove anything."

Prove anything? A couple of years ago, maybe he would have had something to prove. Patrick could still remember the terror that used to make him shake at just the thought of swimming. But not anymore.

"Let me go!" insisted Patrick.

"No, you hold still." Jefferson was far too strong for Patrick, and it hurt where the older boy squeezed his arm tightly. "Go out there and you'll get yourself drowned."

"Jeff, listen, I am *not* going out there to drown." Patrick was ready to hit Jefferson, anything to get free. "I'm just going out to see if I can help someone. You would do the same thing if you could swim."

Jefferson's eyes darkened, and he pressed his lips together for a long moment. But at last he let his friend go.

Patrick ran down to the water's edge near the big rocks on the beach and wrestled a weathered piece of driftwood into the surf.

"At least give me a hand," Patrick shouted as he launched the plank out into the water. Becky hesitated, then ran after him. A wave caught Patrick's board just then and pushed Becky backward into the water with a shriek. She gasped for breath as her light blue dress puffed up around her. Patrick ducked his head and closed his eyes, bracing for the hit of cold, salty water.

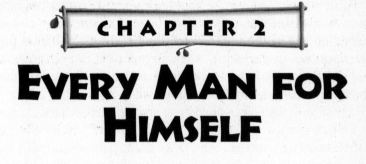

CHAPTER 2

EVERY MAN FOR HIMSELF

Patrick remembered the last time he had found himself in waves like this. The memory of Jefferson washing overboard on the sea journey to Australia still was not a pleasant one, and Patrick shook it from his mind.

Once Patrick had struggled through the first line of huge waves, he paddled with his free arm and kicked as hard as he could toward the ship. He knew there would be rocks just under the surface, and he heard loud sucking noises as the current caught his board and tossed him about. But he gritted his teeth and held on as a lifeboat pulled by, headed toward the shore.

"Hey, there!" shouted Patrick, raising his hand. No one on the boat noticed as they rowed swiftly toward the beach. Patrick counted eight men: One wore a blue captain's uniform, and the others must have been crewmen.

The sailing ship had almost disappeared, leaving behind splintered bits of planks, barrels, and pieces of the masts. Only a small part of the hull survived—what looked like the rear section of the ship, bobbing and thumping up against the rocks. On the deck, two people struggled with a small, upside-down rowboat, trying to get it untied. Patrick felt the tug of a huge wave and pulled back.

"Is anyone else alive out here?" Patrick shouted, almost afraid to ask, but he soon found the answer to his question.

"Bong-cho gul!" came a desperate voice from near the wreck. As Patrick pushed closer, he could see that all around him men clung to the wreckage. Ten, then fifteen, maybe twenty heads bobbed up out of the water like fishing corks. Dark-haired men with dark eyes—some alone, others in groups of two or three—all held silently to bits of the wreck. Most paddled slowly toward shore, while a few others seemed too frightened to move. They all stared at Patrick with wide, fear-filled eyes, and he blinked back.

Patrick pushed closer to the remains of the wreck—the part that bounced against the rocks. Once the two figures on deck had the rowboat free, they loaded a small, finely carved chest aboard, then began to shove the boat into the water. The one man looked somewhat older than Patrick's father. The other, a young boy, must have been a year or two younger than Patrick. Both wore the traditional Chinese man's black long-sleeved blouse and baggy trousers, wet and clinging from the spray.

"Hello, the boat!" Patrick was afraid to paddle closer. He felt the surge of the wave that crashed against the rocks, and it tugged at his legs. The best he could do was watch from a distance.

With the small boat bobbing out in the water, the man turned to the boy and held out his hand. As if slapped in the face, the boy pulled himself back, shook his head, and crossed his arms.

But that was only the beginning of a desperate tug-of-war between the two. The man grabbed the boy's neck, and the boy cried out and tried to get away. They twisted and struggled until the man finally pulled something from the boy's hands, something about the size of a small pear. A little ivory statue? Patrick wasn't sure, but it looked like an animal of some kind. The man laughed as he held the statue in the air, then slipped it into the side pocket of his blouse.

Quick on his feet, he stepped into his boat and slipped the oars into place. The boy tried to follow but misjudged a wave and fell into the water with a splash.

"Ahh!" yelled the boy, grabbing for the back of the boat. But instead of helping him, the man used his oar as a club to bat the boy away.

Some of the other survivors saw what was happening and pointed wildly at the scene with words Patrick could not understand. But no one dared come closer to the rowboat or the doomed piece of ship. The boy was on his own, and the man in the boat swung his oar again and again as he muttered his curses.

"*Wan-nei-chi, kay-chuck-soon*," cried the man, settling back down to his oars. Patrick guessed it meant something like "Get your own boat!" or "Get out of my way!"

Whatever the man had told him, the boy retreated to the wreck. But a wave washed over the top of what was left of the deck, and the boy crouched there with a look of complete terror. He hadn't seen Patrick and made no move to get off to safety.

Whatever is going on? thought Patrick. He had no idea but knew it was certainly not right.

"Stop!" Patrick waved his hands. "You in the boat. Stop!"

But the man in the rowboat was obviously too busy keeping the other survivors away to notice Patrick's feeble shouts. Instead, he pointed to the beach and yelled instructions at them. Patrick didn't understand the words, but the sign language was very clear: *Swim for the beach. Every man for himself.*

As the man left them, Patrick turned his attention back to the wreck and the crying boy. The ship jolted into the rocks one more time with a splintering groan.

It's not going to survive another crash like that, thought Patrick. *And neither is he.*

Whoever *he* was rose to his feet again on the swaying deck and called out, this time in Chinese.

"Jump!" cried Patrick, hoping the boy would understand. "Get out of there!"

The boy finally noticed Patrick, not twenty feet away.

"Might as well be a mile," whispered Patrick, reaching out his hands and motioning for the petrified boy to jump. Another swell was raising up the wreck, and in a moment it would be smashed to kindling.

"Now!" screamed Patrick. "You have to jump! I'll get you."

This time the Chinese boy tried to get away, but there wasn't enough time. The wave picked him up, and the bottom half of the wreck slapped hard against the rock with a horrible crunching and splintering noise. As the wreck twisted for the final time, it catapulted the boy out, barely clear of the flushing waves. If he had been trying to dive, it couldn't have been a finer entry into the water. A moment passed, and Patrick saw a pale hand reach out from the waves.

"I can't get any closer!" cried Patrick, reaching out his hand as far as he could. But he was a couple of feet short, nearly too close to escape the rocks himself. *Just a few more inches.*

Inches from his outstretched hand, Patrick could see the face of the young Chinese boy under the water. Then his head popped up for just a moment and he gasped for air, but the waves pulled him back, claiming a victim.

"No!" Patrick kicked once more to move just a little closer, and the tips of his fingers brushed against a shirt . . . There!

"Got you!" Patrick pulled back and reeled in his catch. His board scraped against something hard, but then they were swept away from the horrible rocks that had cut such a big ship into so much driftwood. And so quickly.

Before he knew it had happened, Patrick was bobbing back with the other wide-eyed survivors, on the beach side of the rocks. The man in the rowboat was far ahead of them, caught in the swells on his way to the beach. And of course the lifeboat with the crew was long gone. The Chinese boy coughed and sniffled and rested his forehead against Patrick's driftwood rescue boat.

"He took it," said the boy.

The words were as clear as the Queen's English, touched only by a faint accent Patrick guessed to be Chinese.

"You speak English?" Patrick asked.

"He took it," the boy repeated again and again, staring straight ahead. "He had no right."

"Are you all right?" Patrick tried once again.

"I must get it back." The boy ignored Patrick's question. "I must. And you will help me."

It was not a question. Patrick wasn't sure why he was going to help the boy get back a little ivory statue, but he was certain from the boy's voice that he'd be helping him.

"Hold on." Patrick felt the wave pick up their board, and they were swept toward shore with the others.

Landing on the beach was not quite as rough as Patrick had feared. With their board they scooted in ahead of the waves and lost themselves in the foam. The next thing Patrick knew, Jefferson's strong hands pulled him out of the water to the safety of the beach.

"Did everybody make it?" panted Patrick. Solid ground felt good, very good, under his feet.

"Don't know for sure." Jefferson looked out at the sea again before turning back to the survivors on the beach. "But I count twenty-five Chinese men, plus the crew, plus—"

Becky helped the coughing Chinese boy to his feet.

"My name is Jasper," the boy answered for himself in a high-pitched squeak, then cleared his throat and lowered his voice. "Jasper Chun."

Finally Patrick got a better look at the boy. Even when Jasper Chun stood up straight, the top of his head came just to Patrick's shoulders. Like most of the other men struggling onto the beach, he looked as if he could use a good meal. His dark, baggy trousers and an even baggier long black shirt flapped like wet flags in the gale.

And his hair! Patrick couldn't stop staring. Jasper's head was shaved around the sides so the jet-black hair looked like a kind of skullcap balanced on top of the boy's head. A single braid hung down in back.

"Twenty-five!" Jasper counted survivors with his skinny finger. The number obviously meant something to him.

"I'm Becky McWaid." Becky offered a smile and a hand to some of the other men who struggled ashore, but most refused her help with a bow of their heads. She pulled back, puzzled.

"The Chinese men," Jasper told her, "will not take help from women. But I thank you, Miss Becky. Everyone made it to the beach."

"Thank God." Becky hugged her shoulders and shivered. So did Patrick.

"He speaks English," Patrick reported the obvious fact to the others. "I don't know if anyone else does. Besides the captain and the crew, I mean."

"Jefferson Pitney." Jeff held out his hand, and Jasper bowed respectfully. Jeff looked at his empty hand for a moment, then scratched his head.

"The captain and his crew are over there." Becky pointed to the far end of the beach, where the ship's lifeboat had been pulled up onto the sand.

"They landed a couple of minutes ago," reported Jefferson. "And they're pulling things out of the water. But it doesn't much look like they want to say howdy."

Patrick squinted at the sailors and remembered how they had surfed past him in the lifeboat.

"We are not important to them," whispered Jasper, crossing his arms and shivering. He spoke as if the men down the beach would hear him. "That is what the captain said when he was leaving us out there. We have lost everything. Now we are just cargo."

Jasper shivered and pointed at the wreck, at the fury of the wind and the waves, and Patrick knew just a small, salty taste of the nightmare this boy had come through. Maybe they had all made it ashore. But was there a brighter side? Patrick wasn't sure. "At least the captain didn't beat you with an oar the way that other fellow did." Patrick looked around the beach to see what had become of the cruel Chinese man. "Who was that?"

"That is Mr. Li, and if you know what is good for you, you will stay away from him."

Patrick looked at Mr. Li's rowboat, which had turned upside down at the foot of the rocks. It had obviously flipped in the waves. As the dripping Mr. Li found a perch partway up the dry side of the rocks, he pointed for the others to pull his boat up higher on the sand.

"Looks like he's in charge," noted Patrick. Firestorm reappeared and began yapping at the growing group of Chinese men huddled around the rocks and the upturned boat.

"There you are!" Patrick ran over to his dog. "We were wondering what happened to you, boy."

"Watch out for Mr.—" But Jasper's warning came too late.

CHAPTER 3

THE SEARCH

"Dog!" The older man kicked angrily at the mutt as Firestorm hopped up to greet him. Firestorm yipped and skittered away, narrowly escaping the man's foot.

"You can't do that!" yelled Patrick, but Mr. Li ignored him and commanded one of the men in Chinese. The younger man reached for Firestorm and fell to the sand. Again the mongrel was too quick.

"What's he doing that for?" Patrick asked Jasper, chasing the dog with the others. "What did he say?"

"Mr. Li said he wanted something to eat," Jasper explained, and finally Patrick understood. He lunged and caught up to Firestorm, gathering him up in his arms. The dog greeted him with a wiggle and a friendly lick on the nose.

"Tell him he can't have Firestorm for dinner." Patrick held his dog tightly and glared at the man.

"Foolish boy," grunted the old Chinese man in English. He didn't speak as clearly as Jasper, but he was not hard to understand. "Dogs make good dinner."

"Not *this* dog," replied Patrick, letting his pet down carefully. "Stay close, Firestorm."

But Firestorm was having too much fun barking and licking the survivors to give up the game. A couple of men petted the animal, but most of them kept their distance and did what Mr. Li told them to do. Mostly they tried to fish floating pieces of wreckage from the waves. Patrick kept a close eye on his pet.

"Mr. Li is in charge of our group," announced Jasper, who had come up obediently to join them. "He paid for our trip here from Canton. That is why we all promised to work for him in the Ballarat goldfields."

"Forever?" asked Patrick, raising his voice against the sound of the waves.

"Oh no." Jasper shook his head seriously. "Not long. For three years only."

Patrick thought that three years of work sounded like a long time to pay for passage from China to Australia. It was a long trip, but not nearly as long as the voyage from Ireland.

"Say," Patrick asked Jasper, remembering the tug-of-war out on the stricken ship. "What did this Mr. Li take from you out there?"

Jasper pressed his fine lips together and looked up at Mr. Li out of the corner of his eye. Mr. Li wouldn't be able to hear them.

"All I have left," whispered Jasper. "A bear statue."

Patrick squinted and wrinkled his nose. "Did you say a bear?"

"My father," continued Jasper, "is here in Australia. He sent it to me and my family."

"That was a nice gift."

"No, you do not understand. His note said it would help us come to be with him here in Australia. I thought he would send money for us in China, but instead the bear. A 'ko-alla,' he called it. His note said that my mother would understand."

"What would she understand?" asked Patrick.

Jasper shrugged his shoulders and shook his head sadly. "Every night after I clean the sailors' rooms in the ship, I dream of finding the answer. Sometimes it seems as if the statue talks to me in the dream, but I cannot understand the words. I wish my mother . . ."

Jasper dropped his eyes. "She died before it came. She never read the note or saw the ko-alla."

"I'm sorry," said Becky quietly.

"I *knew* it wasn't right," fumed Patrick, thinking again of the tug-of-war scene on the sinking boat. Now it started to make more sense. "Mr. Li's a thief. He took what's yours. But why?"

Jasper shrugged. "He does not want any of his people to own pretty things, no matter what. I saw him take a carved pipe from one of the men the first day of our trip. Other things, too."

"That's not right."

"Not right, no." Jasper shook his head. "But we will wait for the right time to get the ko-alla bear back. Then you will help me?"

"No, Patrick," whispered Jefferson. "We'd best let these people work it out among themselves."

"I'll help you." Patrick set his jaw. This time he wasn't going to stand back. He had done that too many times before. Not again. He turned and climbed up to face the king of the beach.

"Wait—not yet!" Jasper tried to hold Patrick back by the sleeve, but Patrick's mind was made up.

"Mr. Li?" Patrick climbed up to where the Chinese man sat, but Mr. Li just ignored him and shouted at his men. Patrick might just as well have been invisible. He swallowed hard and tried again.

"Excuse me, Mr. Li." This time Patrick raised his voice above the whistling of the wind, as if that would help. "You speak English, don't you?"

No answer. Mr. Li waved at a man dragging a broken barrel from the surf. He pointed to where he wanted the man to drop his load.

"Well, sir," continued Patrick, "you have something that belongs to our friend."

The wind blew wisps of the man's graying hair and whiskers around his face and back behind his head. It made him look even older than he probably was.

"Patrick." Becky sounded worried behind him. But he had started this and was going to keep on until the man noticed him.

"I saw you take it. You took Jasper's statue," Patrick continued. "How could you—"

Patrick lost what he was saying when Mr. Li slowly turned his head toward Patrick and stared down at him through half-closed eyes.

"Your Irish nose best stay out of Chinese business," pronounced the man.

"Patrick, come on." This time Becky tugged at Patrick's sleeve. "We can tell Pa."

That's right, we could, thought Patrick. *But I'm here now.*

He cleared his throat. "Yes, well, excuse me, Mr. Li, but I was wondering if you could, well, give it back. It belongs to Jasper, and—"

Mr. Li interrupted Patrick with his crooked smile. One of his top front teeth was missing. The rest were yellow and stained.

"Did Jasper tell you he owe Mr. Li money for passage?" The man talked about "Mr. Li" as if he were someone else.

Patrick nodded.

"Then everything Jasper has," continued the man, "belongs to Mr. Li until Jasper pays off price. Four years."

"Jasper said it was only three."

Mr. Li started to chuckle, and it grew into a long, bumpy laugh. "Four years, three years, all the same. Because even Jasper belongs to Mr. Li, so his pretty statue belongs to me, too. Maybe I give it back when he pays me. Or maybe not. I keep it safe for Jasper."

As the man spoke, he jammed his hand into the pocket where he had put the statue. But his face clouded over, and he looked down in shock at his empty hand.

"Patrick, get down from there." Becky pulled her brother backward off the rock as Mr. Li jumped like a cat from his perch.

Mr. Li snapped his fingers and asked a nearby man a sharp question in Chinese. By the way he said it, Patrick couldn't help thinking it was something like "Give it to me!" or "Where is it, you imbecile!"

The man could only bow and look around helplessly on the sand. Finally he held up his hands. Mr. Li swatted him on the side of the head and barked an order to the other men standing nearby.

"The statue!" Jasper turned to the others. "They have dropped it somewhere."

"Dropped it?" asked Patrick. "How could they do that?"

"Maybe when the rowboat turned over coming in to the beach. Mr. Li had it in his pocket."

Mr. Li wasted no time as he directed his men. With grunts and hand signals, he pointed here and there at seashells and other small rocks. Jasper himself fell to his knees, letting the waves wash over him as he dug through the sand around the boat and muttered to himself. Becky, Jefferson, and Patrick joined in the search, too.

This statue must be pretty special, thought Patrick several minutes later. He reached down into a pool of seawater next to the larger rock, which was about twenty or thirty feet tall. As he searched even deeper, a wave washed over his arm, the power of the tide surging into the pool.

"Oh!" Patrick cried out as he suddenly found himself up to his shoulders in seawater. For a moment he imagined some kind of sea creature below the rock pulling him under.

Patrick stood back up. He watched as waves washed in from the sea, flooded the pool, thrust in under the rock, and then spit out again with a loud sucking sound. It could have been a small cave, maybe, carved into the rock by the waves.

"It's not here," Jefferson called out from the spot where Mr. Li's boat had overturned on the beach. "I sure don't know where your statue is, but it's not here. We've covered the whole beach."

Jasper wasn't about to give up, but after ten more minutes, it was obvious that Jefferson was right. With a nod of his head, Mr. Li signaled his men to stop searching.

"Maybe we can come back and look again," Patrick whispered to Jasper as they stepped back from the waves.

"Your statue probably got lost out there." Jefferson pointed out to sea, then clapped the sand from his hands. "Could try diving for it, I suppose, but the tides run swift around here. It's probably long gone."

"I'm sorry, Jasper," said Becky.

Jasper looked as if he had just lost his best friend. He stood with his arms crossed and eyes closed, leaning up against one of the big rocks. The waves swirled around his ankles, and Patrick wished there were something he could do.

CHAPTER 4

EMPEROR LI

"There on the beach!" shouted a small voice. Patrick turned to see Michael perched on the front seat of a wagon, leading a rescue party of horses, men, and another wagon. Michael was waving wildly, shouting and pointing down at the beach.

"Pa!" Becky ran toward Mr. McWaid, who vaulted out of the lead wagon and bounded down to the beach. He looked very much like his two oldest children, with a slender build and strong, alert eyes. He, too, had curly fire-red hair and a matching, can't-miss-it beard.

"Are you children all right?" He put his arm around Becky.

"I told him what happened," announced Michael. "But where did all these Chinese men come from? Look, they really have pig-tails, just like I've seen in pictures."

"Michael, hush." Becky patted her brother's head. "They're from the ship. Everyone is all right, thank heaven. Just scared, mostly."

"And wet," added their father. "Like you, Patrick. Whatever happened to you?"

"He was just trying to help, sir." Jasper stepped up to Mr. McWaid. "He saved my life."

"I don't think so." Patrick made a circle in the sand with the toe of his wet shoe. "You would have found a way back to shore. There were plenty of boards to float with. It wasn't far."

"Far enough," replied Jasper.

"Well, then, where is the captain?" asked Mr. McWaid. By that time the master of the wrecked ship had found his way down the beach toward them. Mr. Li stood back away from the crowd, and the Chinese men separated to both sides as the captain presented himself.

"What took you so long?" the captain growled, stepping up to face Mr. McWaid. He hiked his ample, round belly over his belt and curled the ends of his mustache with his tongue.

"We came as soon as we heard," explained Mr. McWaid. "My son here ran for help."

"Well, it wasn't soon enough," complained the captain. "When our rudder post snapped, this gale shoved us into those underwater rocks out there."

"But what happened to your ship?" asked Mr. McWaid.

"Isn't it obvious?" The captain's eyes misted over as he stared out to sea. "The old girl turned into firewood just like *that*." He snapped his fingers to make his point.

"But everyone is accounted for," said Becky. "Are they not?"

The beach by that time was littered with splintered bits of lumber, ripped pieces of canvas sail, and broken barrels. Much of it had been dragged in by the sailors and Mr. Li's men. But there wasn't much left to show that there had been a sailing ship out there only minutes before.

"All here," replied the captain. "Seven crew and meself."

"No." Patrick's father looked confused. "I think my daughter is speaking about all the rest of these people."

"Oh, the cargo, you mean." The captain waved his hand at the Chinese men as if he were bothered by a sand flea. "That's Li's affair."

"Lee who?" Mr. McWaid didn't understand.

"*Mr.* Li," Patrick told his father in a low voice. "Jasper says he paid the passage for all these Chinese men. They work for him. He's kind of a . . . a slave owner."

Mr. McWaid nodded and arched his eyebrows. "I see."

"All right, into the wagons, boys." The captain scanned the

beach again and looked as if he would cry. "Figeroa, choose some-one to stay here with you and gather up what you can. Shoot any-one who tries to make off with anything, understand? *Especially* any Chinese."

A large sailor wearing a dirty blue jersey and a frown grabbed the man next to him.

"Aye, Captain. We'll take care of things."

Patrick gulped as the two marched off and the rest of the sailors climbed obediently into the two wagons. The captain wasn't kid-ding, and the sailor's pistol made him look like a pirate.

"What about all these other men?" asked one of the drivers. "We came here for survivors."

The captain shook his head. "Let 'em walk. I've done what Li paid me to do. Got 'em to Australia. Now, look at this sorry mess. I'm going to find me a dry place to stay and count up what we've lost."

"But most of the Chinese men look really weak," Patrick stam-mered and bit his tongue. "They're all wet and cold, and they need to get out of the wind before it's dark. So—"

"You listen to me, lad." The captain spit something dark into the sand at Patrick's feet. "This bunch is trouble, I'm telling ye. Just look at their skin. Smallpox, probably. Yellow fever, maybe even."

"Yellow fever?" The man at the reins of the first wagon pulled back as if he had been hit by a brick. "No one said anything about yellow fever."

"Just wait a minute." Mr. McWaid came to stand next to Patrick. "We're here to help all of these men."

"Help?" The captain threw up his hands. "We could've used some help when we were burying Chinese out there in the South China Sea. *That* would've been a good help."

"That is not true," said Jasper. "None of us was even sick." But his voice was swallowed by the wind.

By this time the captain wasn't listening to anyone anymore. He hopped up into the lead wagon.

"Let's go, men," the captain shouted. "We've had enough of this place and this yellow fever."

That's not fair! thought Patrick, looking back at the crowd of Chinese men. They would not understand the words, but they could see what was happening as well as anyone.

"No offense, mister." One of the drivers looked to Mr. McWaid with a pained look on his face. "But no one told us there were sick people here. We can't take a chance."

The captain's wagon wheeled around and headed slowly away from the ocean, but the man at the reins of the other rig looked back and forth between the captain and Mr. McWaid. Patrick took his chance to jump in front of the wagon.

"Wait just a minute!" Patrick held up his hands. "We don't know if anyone's sick or not. At least we should get the injured Chinese men a ride back to town."

One of the sailors grabbed a whip and held it up. "You heard the captain, boy!" He sneered at Patrick. "Let 'em walk. Or better yet, they can just go back where they came from."

Patrick stood his ground while his father tried his best to hold back the horses. But one of the animals panicked and reared up, kicking its front legs wildly in the air.

"Are you crazy?" the sailor yelled at Patrick. "Get out of the way! We're going to tip over!"

"Patrick!" screamed Becky. The snap of the whip sounded like a shot, and Patrick felt something strike across his back like a flash of lightning.

"Ohh!" Patrick couldn't remember feeling pain like that before. He rolled in agony in the sand as the wagon pulled away.

"Are you all right?" Becky kneeled at her brother's side. There was nothing to do about the pain; Patrick just tried to hold the tears back.

"I . . . I don't know." Patrick squeezed his eyes shut as his father gently peeled back his shirt.

"You had no cause to do that!" Mr. McWaid yelled at the retreating wagon.

But the sailor only laughed as the wagon disappeared back over the dunes.

"Barely nicked you," said Jefferson with an admiring whistle. "You would have felt it if he'd *really* connected."

"Feels as if he did," groaned Patrick. The pain shot through his shoulder.

"That's quite a welt," said Mr. McWaid.

"Ah, it's nothing," continued Jefferson. "Had a rope burn once, looked worse than that. Took weeks to get better. Burned like fire and brimstone."

"Thanks for the word of encouragement." Patrick winced as his father pulled the shirt back down, and Jasper stepped over to see.

"You stay back!" warned Jefferson, and Jasper froze in fear.

"Jeff!" Becky looked at their friend with a puzzled expression. "What's come over you?"

"Nothin's come over *me*." Jefferson stood like a shield between Patrick and Jasper. "And it's nothing personal. No offense to Jasper, but I'm just wondering if maybe what the captain said about the fever might not be true. 'Cause if it is—"

"Jasper can explain," put in Patrick, but Jefferson wouldn't budge.

Jasper bowed stiffly and backed away. "Three sailors already died at sea. They were not Chinese, of course. I had to take them water in their beds. They were burning up with fever."

"I still don't like this. . . ." Jefferson kept his arms crossed. "The fever."

"Listen," said Mr. McWaid. "Sick or no, these men need a place to stay. We'll take them to town, get them dried out and fed, at least, before they go on their way. "

"I want to stay here," announced Jasper, looking back at the ocean.

"But you need to come back with the rest of us," insisted Becky. Jasper shook his head.

"We'll help you look for your koala statue again later," said Patrick. "I promise."

Becky took the boy's elbow as they started away from the ocean.

They were stopped by a piercing command.

"Boy Jasper!" shouted Mr. Li. It was the first they had heard from him since the captain and his crew left the beach. He rattled off a string of Chinese words that ended with something like "You carry!"

Carry? wondered Patrick. His back still burned like a torch, but he tried to ignore it. When he turned he saw two of the Chinese men had put together a kind of stretcher with pieces of broken barrel boards and four long poles tied into a crude frame. Mr. Li was pointing at one of the four pole ends.

"I sit," said Mr. Li, settling down to a crouching position on the board. "You carry."

So that's it, thought Patrick. *Mr. Li acts like the emperor of China, and now he wants to be carried like the emperor.*

Patrick waited breathlessly to see what Jasper would do.

"Hurry, boy," insisted Mr. Li. Patrick wondered why the man bothered to speak to him in English. "Do not forget, Mr. Li owns you."

Jasper clenched his fists and stood his ground.

"Don't worry, Jasper." Patrick stepped up closer. "I'll help you lift it."

But that was the wrong thing to do. Jasper's face turned stormy, and he stood up straight.

"I'm not a little child," he announced, his face red. "I can do it myself."

Jasper brushed Patrick aside, stepped over to the emperor carrier, and lifted a corner with three other Chinese men. Jasper was short, but not much shorter than the others, so the carrier was only a bit off balance. Mr. Li smiled with pleasure and kept up his sharp instructions.

"Higher there," he ordered Jasper. "No bumping."

"That's it, then," sighed Mr. McWaid. "Let's help the others back to town as best we can. When we get closer, I'll go ahead and see if we can find them a place to stay. A barn, perhaps."

Becky nodded in agreement. "As long as that captain fellow

hasn't warned everyone in town that the yellow fever is invading."

Patrick shuddered to think what would happen when they made it back to town. He had a sinking feeling it wouldn't be a friendly welcome.

CHAPTER 5

NO WELCOME

"Isn't that getting heavy?" Michael asked Jasper. "Can you carry it all the way back to Goolwa?"

With the pole on his shoulder, Jasper had already stumbled several times. Mr. Li stared straight ahead from his grand throne, keeping his balance, ignoring their talk.

"Not heavy," said Jasper. His face was red. He pinched his lips together and shook his head. "Not heavy at all."

"I don't believe you," Michael replied.

Still Mr. Li kept up his royal stare, ignoring them all.

"So you're really all from China," Patrick blurted out, trying to keep the conversation going. "I've never met anyone from China."

Jasper didn't seem to mind the obvious question, though his soft voice was hard to hear.

"See Yap District, Guangdong Province," he said. "That is where we come from."

"And your family?" wondered Becky. "What about them?"

That would be a harder question to answer, Patrick could tell. Jasper took another deep breath and continued.

"My mother and brothers all died in China." Jasper closed his eyes for a second. "Missionaries who taught me Jesus and English, they died, too. Only my father and I are left. But my father came here to Australia, and he does not know what has happened."

The way Jasper told it, the story could have been a page from a history book. A simple fact, just like the year was 1869 or that Goolwa was at the mouth of the Murray River. But then he blinked back the tears, and it turned into more than just a story.

"This salt air and the wind," explained Jasper, "they make my eyes burn."

"Mine too." Patrick nodded and wiped his eyes with the wet sleeve of his shirt. "But what about your father? You mentioned he was here in Australia?"

"Ballarat. My father is in the Ballarat goldfields. He is waiting for me there."

Patrick pictured a spot on the map of Australia, halfway between Echuca and the southern coast. Ballarat was the lively gold rush town in the hills, miles away from the river. It grew into a boomtown when gold was discovered there about fifteen years ago. But the gold had disappeared almost as quickly as it had been discovered. Sure, people still found a nugget here and there—enough to make the occasional newspaper headline, but not enough to make many people rich. Did Jasper know the gold was already gone in Ballarat? Patrick wondered and leaned closer to hear the boy's story.

"The captain of the ship." Jasper pointed with his chin in the direction the sailors had taken. "He promised to unload us in Robe. We would walk to the goldfields from there. Even though I have to work for Mr. Li, I would see my father again. I have not seen him since . . . many years."

"You must miss him." Becky looked as if she understood. Jasper nodded and looked around at the sandy hills.

"So where is this Robe?" Jasper interrupted Patrick's thoughts. Jasper pronounced the name of the seaside town like a judge's robe.

"You mean ROW-bee?" Becky pronounced the name the way Patrick had heard the local Australians say it. "They say Robe's quite a few miles down the coast. Down the peninsula. I'm afraid you're not even close. You'll have to walk a ways if you're going to Robe."

"I see." Jasper turned to the man walking beside him and told him something in Chinese. The man groaned and looked up fearfully at Mr. Li.

As they walked, Becky pulled Patrick back to ask him a question. "Do you think something is . . . well, odd about Jasper?"

"I didn't notice."

"His voice—don't you think it's different?"

Patrick shook his head. "Maybe it's because we've never known a Chinese boy before. Maybe all Chinese boys sound like Jasper."

"Maybe." Becky shook her head. "But I don't think so. There's something else. I just don't quite know what it is yet."

"Well, let me know when you find out. I think he's a nice fellow."

"I didn't say he wasn't nice. There's just something he's not telling us."

"So you think he's a mysterious Celestial." Becky didn't respond to Patrick's use of the name for Chinese that he had seen in a newspaper. Michael took the chance to change the subject.

"I think we should call it Koala Beach," he announced as he stepped on the heel of Patrick's boot.

"What are you talking about?" Becky looked over her shoulder at her youngest brother.

"I said, I think we should call it Koala Beach." Michael was always naming places. "Didn't you say the Chinese fellow lost a bear statue there?"

"Call it whatever you like, Michael. We don't know its *real* name."

"Koala Beach *will* be its real name." Michael smiled impishly and ran to Jasper's side to tell him the news. They were just about the same height, and Michael grinned as if they shared a secret.

Jefferson only frowned at the sight and kept his distance from the rest of them, off to the side, as they continued on. Mr. McWaid hurried on ahead to make arrangements for a place to stay.

"We're almost there," said Patrick as the ragged party approached the town. The wind had died down a bit as they made their way from the beach, and Patrick's stiff, salty clothes were slowly drying. He shook the sand out of his hair and turned his head sideways to drain the last of the seawater from his ears.

"Almost there," Michael echoed.

But as they entered Goolwa, Patrick imagined his worst fears were coming true. People stopped what they were doing and stared from their doorsteps at such an odd parade. Many of the doors slammed shut. Horses stopped short in the dusty street. Even the workers on the waterfront—tough men who were used to anything—stopped what they were doing to watch. No one said a word.

"What are they all staring at?" wondered Michael. "Haven't they ever seen Chinese people before?"

Maybe they just haven't seen the emperor, thought Patrick. Mr. Li didn't seem to care about the oddity of four men carrying him on their shoulders while everyone else walked. He just stared straight ahead, his hands folded, like a king entering a conquered city.

"I hope Pa found them a place to stay," Becky worried as they neared the railroad tracks and the wharf.

"Well, they're sure not all going to fit on the *Lady E*." Patrick checked the lineup of paddle steamers. Some were tied up at the wharf. Others, like theirs, were anchored out in the river, not far from shore.

"Clumsy!" Mr. Li shouted as they crossed the railroad tracks. "You will make me fall."

Three of the men holding him up struggled under the weight, but Jasper had fallen on his face in the gravel.

"Jasper!" Becky fell to her knees to help him up, but he would not move. It took Patrick, Becky, and Michael to roll him over.

"Take a rest," Becky urged him. She sounded just like her mother would have.

"You don't look so good, Jasper." Michael fanned the boy's face with his hand. Jasper's cheeks were cherry red, and he gasped for breath.

"Will look worse if he does not pick up his corner." Mr. Li wasn't going to give up his position easily.

"Don't you see he can't go on?" Patrick asked, looking up at the man. "He can't carry you anymore."

Jasper tried to stand up again, but this time Becky held him down.

"No," she whispered. "That's enough. You can't do this."

"It's all right." Mr. McWaid stepped up, arriving from the direction of the waterfront. Over Mr. Li's surprised grunts, he slowly helped the other three Chinese men lower the carrying seat. "We're here now. And I think you can walk just fine, Mr. Li. In this country, we all know how to walk."

"But—" Mr. Li's eyes popped out in surprise as Mr. McWaid continued in his gentle Irish way.

"In fact, sir, I've taken the liberty of finding you and your people a dry place to stay for the night. Won't cost you a thing. It's just over here."

"I—" Mr. Li still hadn't found his tongue.

"Oh, you don't need to thank me." Mr. McWaid's eyes twinkled in the day's last sunshine as it reflected off the river. "You can thank the fellow who owns the warehouse. He says you're welcome to bed down for the evening."

With a weary smile Mr. McWaid led them across the railroad tracks to a ramshackle warehouse on the waterfront. What was left of the paint was peeling badly, most of the shingles were blown away, and the top of the roof looked like an old swaybacked horse. But the hard-packed dirt floor was swept and dry. A few wooden boxes and old wool bales lined the walls, casting shadows between them. Plenty of room to lie down.

"We can stay here?" asked Jasper. He had dragged the last few yards to the warehouse with his arm around Becky's shoulder.

"I'm going to sleep on this," said Michael, bouncing up and down on a wool bale not far from the large double doors. It actually looked fairly soft and inviting, and it was as big as they were.

"Oh no, you're not." Patrick pulled his brother away. "We're going back out to the *Lady E*."

"Jasper," called Michael, "you should try this. It's nice and soft. Really. Like a feather bed."

Jasper waved and smiled at them but found his own spot on a pile of canvas in a dark corner. The other Chinese men filed in quietly. The only one who raised his voice was Mr. Li, demanding that two of his men build him a mattress out of half-empty sacks of grain.

"There's a barrel of water just outside," announced Mr. McWaid. "And we'll see about getting you all some food. In the meantime, I think for your own safety, you'd better stay in the warehouse."

"Thank you." Jasper's voice sounded weak and very far away.

Patrick took his brother's hand and led him outside to the waterfront. Jeff was already waiting for them in a rowboat, looking cross.

"Let's get back out to the *Lady E*," Jefferson said. He pushed off the boat before Patrick even had a chance to sit down.

Patrick wasn't sure why he woke up so early the next morning. Church wasn't until much later. It wasn't the sun, which still only cast shy hints of gold in the eastern sky. And it probably wasn't the paddle steamer's squeaks, the slap of waves on the hull, or the cry of a bird outside. Patrick had come to love the night sounds of the sleeping *Lady Elisabeth*.

I can't sleep anyway, he told himself, his eyes wide open. His back still throbbed a bit from the lashing. It was hard to roll over.

So he rose silently from his bedroll, pulled on his clothes, and stepped carefully over Becky and Michael. Jeff still snored up in his usual spot on the floor of the wheelhouse. Mr. and Mrs. McWaid were asleep in the captain's room. Even Christopher the koala was snoozing, while Firestorm was having a dog dream, twitching his legs and woofing softly. Patrick figured they wouldn't wake for another hour or two. Maybe he could use the time to be quiet, to pray. Early mornings were a good time for that.

Ahh. Out on the deck he took a deep breath of sweet river air, this morning laced with a hint of tangy ocean from across the peninsula. His favorite smell. And he smiled at the feel of cool dew under his bare feet. Only the gentlest of breezes ruffled the dark surface of the river between where they floated at anchor and the deserted Goolwa waterfront. But was it quite deserted? A movement between two buildings caught his eye.

Who could that be? he wondered. *Nobody else is awake yet.*

But somebody *was* awake, and whoever it was slipped from behind the old warehouse where Jasper and his Chinese friends were sleeping. In fact . . . Patrick squinted. . . .

That's Jasper!

Patrick stared across the water as Jasper slipped past the railroad tracks and padded down the street, away from town. Patrick thought about calling out, but only for a moment.

Where's he going?

Patrick slipped quietly into their rowboat and untied it as quickly as he could. Never mind his growling stomach.

No matter where this fellow goes, he promised himself, *I'll be back to the boat by breakfast.*

A faint scuffling noise up on deck made the hair on the back of his neck stand up.

"Who's there?" Patrick whirled to see who might be following him.

CHAPTER 6

DARK DANGER

Patrick had to smile when he saw a cocked head with perky ears, peering down at him from the deck.

"Firestorm!" he whispered. "You stay there. I'll be right back."

But Firestorm had other ideas. He barked once as he crouched low and swept the deck with his tail.

"No!" hissed Patrick. "Shh!"

That was all Firestorm needed, and he launched himself into Patrick's arms.

"Oh, you!" Patrick knew he had lost the argument, so he settled his dog in the front of the boat as best he could, pushed away from the *Lady E*, and pulled for the Goolwa wharf. Firestorm sniffed eagerly at the air ahead, like a living figurehead.

"I have a feeling I know where Jasper's going," Patrick whispered to his dog. Firestorm replied with a *thump-thump* of his tail. "Koala Beach."

But by the time they had made it to shore, Jasper was already out of sight down the street. They would have to hurry to catch up with him.

"Come on!" Patrick turned and ran, and Firestorm followed his master like a shadow. They trotted through the streets in the same direction Jasper had taken.

"Jasper!" Patrick called, but he wasn't sure if the other boy had heard him. "Jasper, wait for us!"

Patrick's clothes weren't damp anymore, but the dried sea salt in them from the day before made his legs sting with every step. He slowed to a walk, but it still hurt. And the welt on his back was throbbing again.

"I don't know why I'm doing this, boy." Patrick looked down at Firestorm, who tipped his head curiously to the side. "But we can't just let him run out alone, can we?"

Patrick shuddered when he remembered how the captain of the smashed ship had told his two men to "shoot anyone who tries to make off with anything" from Koala Beach. He wondered if that included boys who went back looking for ivory statues.

Firestorm ran ahead as if he knew the way. Patrick followed as fast as his aching legs would take him, retracing their steps from the day before.

Here we go again, he told himself. The beach hadn't seemed as far away the day before. Just a short walk across the peninsula.

Maybe so, but Patrick was huffing for breath as he crested the last few dunes. The sand tugged at his feet.

"Jasper must have been quick," he told the dog. "The only things we caught up to were his footprints in the sand."

Firestorm looked back and eagerly wagged his tail, looking for another game on the beach.

"Hold on, boy. You don't want those two sailors to see us." Patrick grabbed Firestorm by his rope collar, and they crouched just below the crest of the last sand hill before Koala Beach. What had happened to Jasper?

Maybe he's not even here.

But he *was*. As Patrick slowly peeked over the hill at the beach, he could see Jasper kneeling in the sand at the water's edge, near the large rocks. The gale from the day before had died down a bit, and Patrick noticed more of the rocks were exposed.

Besides that, the beach was now nearly covered with wreckage from the dead ship. More old sails, pieces of cork, bottles, boards, and barrels. Not much to guard, as far as Patrick could tell. Down by the water, Jasper picked up a stick that had drifted to his side and threw it into the waves.

That was enough for Firestorm; he yanked free from Patrick's grip and went skittering down the face of the hill to greet Jasper and fetch the stick.

"Firestorm!" Patrick whispered and scrambled after the dog. That's when he saw the guards, fast asleep in the shelter of a couple of boards and a smoldering fire, beyond the reach of the waves. But they were farther off to the right, on the other side of the big rocks.

They're going to wake up. Then what?

Patrick didn't like the idea of going down on the beach again, but he hurried to join Firestorm and their Chinese friend. Jasper jumped and yelped when Patrick tapped him on his shoulder.

"In China we do not startle people like that!" he said, wiping a tear from his eye. "It is rude."

"Shh." Patrick nodded and put his finger to his lips. "I'm sorry. But the guards over there beyond these rocks—I don't think they'd be too happy if we woke them up."

"They cannot see us. And I do not care."

"Well, you should. You heard what the captain said about shooting anybody who tries to come back here or take away things from the wreck."

"They do not have to worry." Jasper frowned and threw a handful of sand at the water. "The statue is not here. I have looked everywhere. It must have fallen in the water and been carried out to sea."

Patrick knew Jasper was probably right. Even with the light from a hazy, rising sun, they could search for weeks and not find the treasure. Patrick picked up an opened jug from the sand.

"What's this?" he asked.

Jasper shrugged. "Water bottle from the ship. I found it floating. Have some."

Patrick sniffed the jug carefully, then took a sip. The water was a little stale, but it seemed fine. Water was better than nothing for his empty stomach, he decided.

"We should go back," Patrick finally said, wiping his lips. "I just came out here with Firestorm to make sure you didn't try to walk by yourself to Robe."

"Firestorm?" Jasper looked around them on the beach.

Patrick groaned. "Not again! That dog is always disappearing."

But this time it wasn't hard to track fresh paw prints through the hard-packed silver sand, farther around the biggest of the rocks on the ocean side. Waves lapped only a few feet away. They were still out of sight of the guards.

"The prints just disappear into this rock!" whispered Jasper, looking down at the sand. "Where did he go?"

"Not into the rock," replied Patrick, stooping down. "*Under* the rock. He's down there in some kind of cave!"

"Are you sure? I did not see a cave there before."

"The tide wasn't so low yesterday. Look, this cave was partly covered with water when we were here before."

Patrick had to get down on his stomach to see, but sure enough, the low tide had revealed an opening under the rock, only a few feet wide and just tall enough to squeeze into on his hands and knees. Actually, it could hardly be called a cave. Just a dark slice of an opening. But why Firestorm was curious enough to even poke his nose in there, Patrick surely didn't know.

"I think we should look inside," Patrick decided, and he whistled softly for the dog to come. Firestorm either didn't hear or didn't want to come out yet.

"I am not going in there," Jasper told Patrick, wrinkling his nose. "It is dark. And it smells like dead fish."

Jasper had a point, and the tide was already coming up again. But what about Firestorm?

"He's going to be trapped in there," worried Patrick, holding his hand down and clapping softly in front of the opening. "Come on, Firestorm, get out now!"

Patrick thought he heard a digging sound and a whimper, but he couldn't be sure, and he definitely couldn't see anything in the dark hole. In the meantime, Jasper had wandered around the rock and came running right back.

"The guards!" he cried, splashing through a shallow wave. "One of them is coming this way!"

Oh no, thought Patrick with a rush of panic. *Where do we go?*

It took only a moment to see that one of the guards was wandering straight for them from the left, the ocean side of the rocks. Well, not *straight* for them; he took the time to stroll around the beach a bit and toss a few stones into the waves. When he yawned and stretched, Patrick was sure he hadn't seen them yet. But there had been *two* guards.

"Figeroa!" came a shout from the other direction, around the right side of the rock. Patrick looked to his right, expecting to see the other guard at any moment.

"Down here!" hissed Patrick. "The guards are coming around from both directions!" He grabbed Jasper's wrist and slithered through the narrow opening on his stomach, into the damp darkness. Jasper didn't need the help. Fish smell or no fish smell, he was coming along.

"I hope there's nothing dead in here," Patrick whispered, but the awful smell that met his nose told him there had to be. There was no way to tell exactly what size their cave was, but it certainly wasn't big.

"I don't like this," Jasper groaned softly, and Patrick put his hand on the boy's mouth as they wiggled farther inside. Patrick knew he and Jasper hadn't done anything wrong by just being on the beach, but he wasn't so sure the guards would know the difference between looters and two boys. Once inside, they were barely able to turn themselves around so they could watch the opening.

"Where are they?" Jasper wondered softly. "Will they not see our footprints? And where is your dog?"

The sound of waves out on the beach seemed louder all the time. The two of them listened, completely still, for any sign of the men outside or the dog inside.

"I don't hear anything," Patrick finally replied. "But don't move."

Yet Patrick couldn't help moving when he felt a warm tongue licking his foot.

"Firestorm!" he whispered. He dug his sandy fingers into his dog's shaggy fur. "What are you doing in here?"

Firestorm just whimpered and wagged his tail happily as they tried to keep still. After another couple of minutes, they finally heard faint voices out on the beach. Patrick thought he saw the shadows of a pair of feet walking by, just outside the cave entry. But no one was crawling in after them. Jasper let out his breath when the feet finally moved away.

"Have you ever been in a cave before?" he asked Patrick, his voice shivering. It sounded as if he was going to cry.

"Once. But this feels more like a tomb than a cave." Patrick kept his eye on the shadowy entry, wondering how soon the waves would reach them.

"I think you are right," whispered Jasper. "I cannot even sit up."

Patrick rolled over on his back and reached up his hand. All he could feel was a soft, dripping ceiling of dark things that smelled horrible and seemed to grab at his fingers.

A tomb. Patrick shuddered. *I hope not*. Something like a wet, sticky sponge brushed against the top of his head.

"Jasper?" Patrick shook his head while he tried not to think of tombs or the smelly tide pool creatures all around them.

"Yes?"

"Tell me more about your family. What's your father like?"

"My father . . ." Jasper paused for a moment. "He used to get on his knees and play with my two little brothers."

Patrick chuckled. "Sounds like my pa."

"He used to make us laugh. Told us stories, too. Bible stories. Until . . ."

Jasper sighed.

"People found out when we became Christians. On the street in Canton, they cursed us, said we betrayed our ancestors. They did not even *know* us, and they spit on us! And my father, they would not let him work anymore. He wanted to, but they beat him instead."

Patrick gulped at the story. Firestorm started digging at their feet, flicking sand in Patrick's face.

"That is why my father came here to Australia," Jasper explained quietly. "To find a new place where we could live without being afraid."

"You found the new place. Now you just have Mr. Li to worry about. He sure wanted that statue of yours, didn't he?"

"Mr. Li." Jasper's voice turned very serious. "When he saw I had the statue, he thought he could sell it for money. That is all he thinks about: money, money, money."

"That, and ordering people around, right?"

"Well, yes. And he tried to take the statue from me many times. So I hid it on the ship. But he noticed it again when we hit the rocks out there."

Patrick remembered the crazy tug-of-war on the deck of the sinking ship.

"Maybe it is not so valuable after all. Just a piece of ivory. But my father wanted us to have it. . . ."

"I understand," answered Patrick. "You don't have to explain anything else." He remembered for a moment the months when their father had been gone, accused of a crime he did not commit and taken on a prison ship to Australia.

This fellow's been through all that I have, Patrick told himself. *And more. At least I still had the rest of my family when we were looking for Pa. Jasper has no one.*

"Listen, Jasper," Patrick finally spoke up again. "I'll be your friend. I don't see how we can find your statue, but you're not far from finding your father. I know what that's like."

"Thank you." Jasper sounded very far away.

As they talked, Patrick wiggled on his back, trying to get clear of a piece of something sharp. Besides the horrible dripping ceiling, the sand on the floor of their tomb was littered with odd, dark things that didn't feel good to lie on or crawl across—driftwood, pieces of the ship . . . who knew? And then there were the soft bodies of dead sea creatures all around them.

They smell dead, anyway.

One of them squirted a foul stream of juice in Patrick's face, and he jerked his head back.

"Ohh," he groaned.

A moment later Patrick decided that squishy, smelly stuff wasn't the worst thing about the cave. A cold wave finally sloshed in, glimmering with an emerald light from outside—just enough to make out a shadow of something moving, something coming at them from inside the cave.

"Get it off me!" shrieked Jasper in a high-pitched whisper that surely could have been heard outside. "A sea creature!"

Patrick reached over to tackle whatever had crawled over Jasper, and Firestorm growled.

"Just a little crab," said Patrick. He let the animal pass by. A noise outside set Patrick on guard. "Quiet!" he whispered.

Again they froze in their hiding place, and a moment later a boot stopped, barely visible in the wet sand outside. Then came another shout, a little louder.

CHAPTER 7

CONSIDER THE RAVENS

Did they hear us? wondered Patrick. At any moment he expected a man's face to appear at the cave opening. Instead, they were hit and soaked by another wave. The pair of feet outside danced out of the way, up onto the rocks.

"I'm going out to check," Patrick finally whispered. He kept his hand on Firestorm's collar.

"No!" Jasper whispered and grabbed him by the back of his shirt. "They could be standing right above the cave opening. If they see your head poking out . . ."

Another small wave hit the opening.

"Listen, the tide is coming in fast," argued Patrick. "We can't just stay here while the cave fills up."

"I know that. But . . ."

They lay quietly in the wet sand, shivering and listening to the waves outside, trying not to move, listening for any sound that would tell them the guards were close by. Firestorm didn't seem to mind the water as he kept splashing and pushing sand in their faces. Digging. Always digging. Yet another wave crashed in, and then another.

"We can't stay in here," said Patrick, rolling over on his stomach. This time he didn't worry about whispering.

Sand and water were flying in Patrick's face. Firestorm kept pulling things up and dropping them for Patrick to share. A stick. A dead fish. An odd-shaped rock. Patrick tossed the rock in Jasper's direction, and it hit the shallow water with a splash. But in the dark, flickering light from the cave opening, Patrick saw Jasper's face brighten. Jasper reached down into the water.

"What is it?" wondered Patrick.

"The statue!" Jasper tried to straighten up but bumped his head. "Ow!"

"You don't mean—"

"Your dog found my statue!" Jasper raised his voice. "Your wonderful dog found my statue!"

"In here?" Patrick's jaw dropped. But there was no time to wonder; the boys were almost floating on their stomachs inside the tiny cave. Another wave surged in, then another, cutting short their celebration. Patrick looked around and bit his lip.

"We can't stay in here any longer, Jasper! The water isn't going away."

"And if the guards are still outside?"

"Do you know how silly that question sounds right now? We'll take our chances."

Even as they spoke, wave after wave surged straight into the tiny cave with a whooshing sound, mixing their hair with the sea sponges on the ceiling.

"The water!" cried Jasper. "Coming so fast!"

With the water now up to his belly, Firestorm finally gave up his game of fetch and whimpered in the corner by their feet.

"Come, Firestorm," ordered Patrick. "We're getting out of here. Now!"

But it would not be quite that easy. For each foot they crawled forward, they were pushed back two, back again to the dark, jagged corners of the cave.

"I do not know how we are going to get out of here," Jasper gasped with panic. "The water keeps pushing me back."

Patrick raised his face to the top of the cave, searching desperately for the two or three inches of air that were left. Jasper was still gripping his statue.

I could use a life ring just now, thought Patrick, but then he realized even a life ring probably wouldn't help them. This time they had to go *down* before they could go back *up*. Down through the water, through the mouth-shaped opening.

"All right," cried Patrick. "All we do is time the waves. The water comes in, we hear that *swoosh* sound, and there's a second or two when we can shoot out through the opening. You first!"

Jasper nodded. "Let's try it."

"One, two, three . . ." Patrick counted and listened for the *swoosh*, then pushed Jasper out when the power of the waves grabbed them. Jasper ducked and disappeared in the swirling foam.

"There you go, Jasper." Patrick gasped and looked over at his dog, paddling wildly. "Now it's our turn, boy."

Patrick held Firestorm tightly to his side and tried to keep the panicked dog from clawing him. He waited for the push of the next wave, then pointed his nose toward the last inch of air they had left.

"Now!" He knew they would not get another chance. The cave would be filled with water in another few moments. He took one last sweet gulp of air, pushed Firestorm underwater ahead of him, and aimed for the opening in the floor.

And he prayed.

The hardest part was holding on to the dog. Pointed toward the light, Patrick felt like a cork being pushed out of a bottle as they shot out into the daylight. The next thing Patrick knew, he was stumbling through breaking waves back onto the beach, still holding Firestorm. He blinked his eyes in the bright morning sunshine.

"We made it, Jasper." Patrick looked around, but Jasper wasn't there. Firestorm choked and coughed, too, until Patrick lifted his dog up to higher ground and let him loose. Patrick didn't mind the spray when Firestorm shook himself dry.

"Jasper, where are you?"

Patrick gulped when he slipped around the rock to the side of the beach, where the guards had been sleeping.

"Jasper?"

Jasper stumbled toward him from the far side of the rock, his face white with fear. A burly guard held him from behind, twisting Jasper's arm roughly around his back. "Thought ye'd gotten away, did ye?" growled the sailor. He shook Jasper until the young boy was trembling on his knees in the sand.

"Leave him be!" insisted Patrick. He took a step forward. "He hasn't done anything wrong."

The sailor stared blankly at him with bloodshot eyes and wagged a pistol in his free hand.

"Oh, so 'e 'asn't, eh?" The man's grin showed several front teeth missing, probably from too many tavern fights. "Well, the captain, 'e says for me to shoot anyone I sees pokin' about the beach tryin' to steal things, see? And looks to me you two are pokin' about. I got me duty."

"Look, we weren't doing anything wrong." Patrick took another slow step toward them. "Jasper just came back for what's rightfully his. Didn't you, Jasper?"

Patrick gave the other boy his best do-what-I-say-and-go-along-with-me look. He hoped Jasper would understand.

"Eh?" The sailor had his finger on the trigger of the pistol. "An' what might that be?"

"Show it to him, Jasper." Patrick signaled with his eyes as he circled around behind the man. The sailor would not be able to keep track of both of them at the same time—not without turning his head back and forth.

"Uh . . ." Jasper still wasn't sure, but slowly he pulled the ivory statue out of his shirt.

Up close over the man's shoulder, the carving took Patrick's breath away. It didn't take a blundering sailor to see that the bear had been carved by a master. Every hair of the animal seemed to stand out. The proportions were perfect. The nose glistened as if the animal were alive. Even the eyes glittered and shone.

"Say, that's quite a carvin' ye got there." The sailor didn't take his eyes off the statue. "Figeroa, come on over here and take a look at this. The captain, he's goin' to be glad we were on duty. Figeroa?"

The sailor looked around for his friend, but Figeroa was nowhere near.

"Ah, never mind," said the man, sucking on his teeth. "Give it to me, then, and maybe I'll forget you were here."

Patrick was ready for the moment when the sailor fixed his eyes back on the treasure and let his pistol drop just a little. With the speed of a cat, Patrick pounced on the hand that held the pistol, twisting it free with a snap.

The man howled in pain and loosened his grip on Jasper's arm for a moment—long enough for the boy to wriggle free and the pistol to drop to the sand.

"You little—"

Without a word Jasper grabbed the weapon where it had fallen in the sand and pitched it with both hands out into the ocean. Patrick just hoped Firestorm wouldn't try to retrieve the gun. And they sprinted away from the howling man—into the arms of the other sailor. Patrick collided with him first.

"Oh!" cried Patrick. He backed up, nearly tripped over Firestorm, and tumbled around the startled man.

"Hold on, you two," sputtered the guard. Patrick was glad the man didn't have another pistol. He and Jasper scrambled over the hill, Firestorm nipping at their heels.

"I must stop for—" Jasper finally stopped running when they were far enough away from the beach to feel safe. Actually, Goolwa was almost in sight. "I must stop for breath. After being on the ship so long . . ."

"I know." Patrick nodded and looked back again to make sure the two sailors weren't following them. "I'm not much of an athlete, either." He rested with his hands on his knees, his chest heaving like Jasper's. But when he looked up, Jasper was swaying again and dropped to one knee.

"Are you all right?" asked Patrick.

"Just feeling a little weak for a moment."

Patrick helped him back to his feet.

"Are you sure you're going to make it to see your father in Ballarat? That's a long way."

"I will make it."

"Well, I was thinking. Why don't you ride with us up the river on our paddle steamer? We'll let you off nearer to the goldfields. It's three hundred miles from here. That way—"

But Jasper just shook his head. "I would like that, but—"

"But what? We could bring you much closer."

"But I still owe Mr. Li my labor."

"Mr. Li!" Patrick kicked at the dust and startled a small flock of jet black crows that were digging at a pile of feathers. "After all this, how can you even travel with him? I'd be worried if I were you."

Jasper shrugged, and Patrick's stomach rumbled. Firestorm returned from digging at something to bark at the birds as they scattered.

"In fact," continued Patrick, "if I was depending on that fellow, I'd be worried for my next meal."

One of the birds gave a loud *ark-ark-ark* call and retired to the far side of the trail to study them with its curious white eyes. Firestorm growled.

" 'Consider the ravens . . .' " whispered Jasper.

"What's that?" Patrick gave Jasper a sideways glance, just as the bird had done. "Crows?"

Jasper shrugged. "It is a Bible verse the missionaries taught me."

"I know it's a Bible verse. But it doesn't have anything to do with Mr. Li or your statue."

Jasper acted as if he had not heard him. " '. . . for they neither sow nor reap; which neither have storehouse nor barn; and God feedeth them.' "

Patrick thought about how God fed the crows; they had been picking at something dead on the trail. But his Bible-quoting Chinese friend still wasn't done.

" 'How much more are ye better than the fowls?' "

"Was that a question?" Patrick wondered as they left the crows behind. This Jasper was full of surprises.

"Perhaps."

"You're a hard one to figure out," Patrick declared. "I never thought I'd meet a Chinese . . . I mean, I wasn't expecting a . . ."

Patrick's voice trailed off when he realized what he was saying. He hadn't meant to. His face turned red.

"You were not expecting a heathen to know Scripture?" By the look on his face, Jasper didn't seem to mind the back-and-forth.

"I'm sorry," murmured Patrick. "I don't mean to offend. I'm still trying to understand you."

At that, Jasper's face clouded over, and he turned his attention back toward the approaching town. They were almost to Goolwa.

What did I say? wondered Patrick.

Jasper lowered his voice. "It is *I* who should be sorry."

"For *what*?"

"I feel badly for deceiving you," whispered Jasper, "but—"

"Deceiving me? You're just talking in riddles."

Jasper nodded seriously and looked down at the dusty road. His tears fell to the dust.

"You must promise not to tell anyone. If Mr. Li should ever find out—"

Jasper would have continued, but loud voices from the waterfront interrupted them. Patrick stopped short, and a shiver went up his spine when he heard the sounds and saw what was happening.

CHAPTER 8

STANDOFF

"Wait a minute." Patrick put out his arm to stop Jasper in his tracks. He lowered his voice. "I don't think we want to go this way."

Patrick pointed to the warehouse where all the Chinese men had been put up for the night. Jasper froze, too, at the sight of three large men planted in front of the door, both of them facing Patrick's father.

"We're trying to be reasonable, McDonald." The first man wagged his finger in Mr. McWaid's face like an angry old teacher lecturing his class. "So don't you tell us this isn't serious."

Even from a distance, Patrick could tell the man had not a single hair on his head. Without a hat, his bald head reflected the early morning light.

"The name's Mc*Waid*," replied Patrick's father, "and I'll thank you to get your finger out of my face."

Mr. McWaid was standing firmly in the shadows of the warehouse doorway, blocking the entrance. But the two men in front of Mr. McWaid weren't backing away.

"Look, it's nothing against you," explained the second man. He turned his head just a bit to show an enormous long sideburn covering most of his cheek, like a trimmed-away half beard. "But yellow fever . . . We don't want our families catching anything. You understand, don't you?"

A third man with a huge bushy beard nodded silently.

"You're just repeating rumors," replied Mr. McWaid. "We don't know for certain it's yellow fever. So why don't we just call the doctor, shall we?"

"Time's past for that," said the bald man. "We've heard what happens when Chinese come. Next it'll be *your* wife and kids."

"Now, listen here, gentlemen." Mr. McWaid held out his hands, palms up. "I don't think—"

"No!" insisted the bald man. "*You* listen. Only safe thing to do now is send these Chinamen right back to where they came from. Why don't you work with us? No one gets hurt."

"Of all the nerve!" This time it was Mr. McWaid's turn to be angry. "Here in broad daylight, you come insisting these men turn around and go back to China? I've never heard of such a thing."

The bald man shrugged. "I'm just saying it would go easier for you if you helped us."

"I am not moving until the doctor or the magistrate tells me to," insisted Mr. McWaid, planting his feet firmly. "And no one is going back to China simply because you say so. Now, if you'll excuse me."

He turned to go, but the man with the sideburns grabbed his shoulder and spun him back around.

"Look, McDonald—"

"It's Mc*Waid*," repeated Patrick's father, and his face looked as red as his beard. "John McWaid, and I'm the skipper of the paddle steamer *Lady Elisabeth*, out of Echuca, and you have no right—"

"Don't talk to us about rights, Mr. Riverboat." The man never backed away a step. "The only right that matters here is the right to protect our lives and our families. You understand that."

"And these men don't have the same right?" Mr. McWaid pointed with his thumb back at the warehouse, where Patrick could see a couple of shadowy forms.

But the men didn't answer Mr. McWaid's question. Firestorm whimpered and looked up at Patrick as if to ask why they were stopping so long.

"Quiet, boy." Patrick bent down to shush his dog without pulling his eyes away from his father.

"We're not here to argue," said the man with the sideburns. "We just want some action. We're just standing up for the decent people of this town!"

"I appreciate that, friend." Mr. McWaid lowered his voice as he tried to turn the men around and head them away from the warehouse. "And you made your point. But we don't need panic just now."

Instead of leaving quietly, though, the men dug in their heels and threw Mr. McWaid's hand from their shoulders. Maybe they realized for the first time that they had an audience; a small crowd of curious people had collected to watch the standoff.

"You don't understand, mister," pleaded the bald-domed man, this time with a good measure of desperation in his voice. "If we don't stop it here, pretty soon the streets will be crawling with Chinese, and who knows what kind of plagues they're bringing. Don't you see? You want that on your head?"

The man waved his hand around the street.

"And what about all you people? You just going to stand here and let this outbreak start from that warehouse? The captain of the wrecked ship said it was yellow fever—or worse!"

No one said a word in the uncomfortable silence that followed. A woman turned to take her young child away. A man coughed and shook his head before turning to go.

They're not cheering him on, thought Patrick. *That's good*.

But then the bald man turned, and his eyes came to rest on Patrick and Jasper, standing dead still in the road. Patrick crouched and put his arms around Firestorm.

"Say." The man pointed at them. "Look there. One of the Chinese. He's already loose on the streets!"

Jasper tried to pull back quietly and disappear into the shadow of a packing shed, but it was too late. First the sailors, now this. What would the two men do? Jasper hesitated for only a moment before he sprang out of the shadows and ran away.

"No!" cried Patrick, stumbling after him. "It's all right, Jasper."

But Patrick knew it wasn't. As the men roared at them to stop, Patrick grabbed at Jasper's shirt and missed. They dove down an embankment toward the river. Jasper stumbled, but Patrick managed to grab him and they rolled down the hill. Jasper was the first one in the water.

We're all wet anyway, thought Patrick as he followed Jasper into the cold river. They made their way toward the anchored *Lady Elisabeth*.

"Come on, Firestorm!" Patrick waved for his dog to follow. Firestorm planted his front paws by the edge of the water, curled, and sprang in after them, ready for another swim.

"See anybody?" asked Jasper once they were a safe distance away from the wharf. With a little help from Patrick, he was paddling with one hand and keeping the ivory statue safe in the other. They weren't moving very fast, but at least Jasper was keeping afloat—barely.

Patrick expected to see the three men from the waterfront chasing them.

"I don't think they came after us." Patrick breathed another sigh of relief as he sighted the bobbing white hull of the *Lady Elisabeth*. It was the third boat from the left in a long lineup of paddle steamers, each one waiting for its turn at the wharf. "And I've had enough of close scrapes for a while."

"You too? What about your father? Do you think he is all right with those three?"

Their question was answered by a whoop, followed by the sound of hooves in the street.

"We'll be back, McWaid!" shouted the lead man. "Mark my words."

Patrick's father said something he couldn't understand.

"Fine with us if you *do* tell the constable, McWaid! Tell the magistrate, too."

The three men on horseback sped away in a cloud of dust. But out in the river Jasper lagged behind, a pained expression on his face.

"Say." Patrick waited for Jasper to catch up. "You don't swim very well."

Patrick thought for a moment about the rowboat he had left tied to the other side of the wharf. He wasn't sure how his father had made it to shore.

"I swim fine." Jasper nodded but barely managed to keep his face above water. He paddled like a dog, splashing them both. "Sometimes, when I was a boy, I swam out to boats in Canton Harbor just like this."

"Just like this?"

"Sure." Jasper coughed and kept paddling.

A couple of minutes later, Patrick flopped onto the deck of the *Lady E* and turned to help Jasper.

"This way up," Patrick grunted, pulling Jasper's hand. Michael appeared behind him to help Jasper and then Firestorm up on deck.

"Where have you been, Patrick?" asked Michael. "We've already had breakfast. Pa yelled at someone to give him and Jeff and Becky a ride to the wharf. They were looking all over for you."

"We were just—"

"You're just going to have some explaining to do," interrupted Mrs. McWaid. The noise must have brought her out of her galley, the paddle steamer's kitchen. She hurried over to Patrick. "We were so worried about you after you disappeared. Where have you been?"

"I'm sorry," whispered Patrick, feeling himself shrink. "I was just helping Jasper—"

"It was my fault, Mrs. McWaid." Jasper stood between the two and bowed. "I was the one who kept Patrick this morning. He was trying to help me. I am very sorry."

"I see. Well . . ." Mrs. McWaid took a step back, but she nodded politely at the newcomer. "They didn't tell me you spoke English so well!"

"Yes, ma'am." Jasper smiled shyly, and Patrick could tell his mother was going to have a hard time staying angry at them, as they followed her into the cramped galley.

"So tell me where you've been all this time," Mrs. McWaid insisted. "You really *did* have us worried."

Patrick and Jasper looked at each other, and Patrick swallowed hard. Should they start with the trouble at Koala Beach, or the trouble they'd just seen on the wharf?

"Well . . ." Patrick began.

"I lost this on the beach," offered Jasper, holding up the statue of the koala. Michael whistled, and Mrs. McWaid's eyes widened a bit, just as the guard's eyes had done back at the beach. "I think it was caught in Mr. Li's boat and then dragged up next to these big rocks. Last night, the waves washed it inside a small cave."

"Firestorm dug it out this morning," added Patrick.

"That's . . ." Mrs. McWaid studied the work of art. "That's remarkable."

"It belonged to my father," explained Jasper. "He sent it to my family. I am going to meet him in Ballarat, even though I hear there is no gold left there."

"I see." Mrs. McWaid nodded politely and returned to cleaning her dishes.

"I wonder what happened to Pa." Michael stood on a box for a better view out a window. Patrick glanced outside to see his father at the oars of a small boat, just pushing away from the wharf.

"Oh, there he is," said Mrs. McWaid. "He must have left Becky and Jefferson on shore. But it looks as if he's bringing someone with him. One of the Chinese men."

Sure enough, Mr. Li was settling into the rear seat of the rowboat, taking up his regal pose, his arms crossed. But when Patrick turned back to tell Jasper, the boy had disappeared.

"Where are you going?" yelled Patrick when he caught sight of Jasper. The Chinese boy was making his way toward the paddle steamer's side deck, facing the approaching rowboat.

"To meet Mr. Li, of course."

"No, no, no." Patrick put a hand to his own forehead and shook his head. "You'll do no such thing. If he sees you, he's just going to take everything you own again. You can't."

"But I owe—"

"Yes, you've said that already. You owe him. I know that. But we're not going to let him take advantage of you. You're going to hide until he's gone; then we'll figure things out."

"I do not think that is wise."

"Wise enough for me. Now, come on."

Patrick felt a bump on the other side of the paddle steamer. The rowboat. Mr. McWaid was there, along with Mr. Li!

"Hurry!" Patrick whispered and pulled Jasper to his feet.

"But I have done enough hiding," protested Jasper. "The last time I hid with you—"

"Shh." Patrick looked around for somewhere Jasper could hide. Not in the wheelhouse—that would be too obvious. Maybe in the engine room. But they would have to pass through the salon to get there. Mr. Li was probably already climbing up on the opposite deck. Too late for that. There was only one choice left.

"Here you go." Patrick handed Jasper the end of a rope and threaded the other end through a wooden toe railing. Jasper tried to protest one more time.

"I still do not think I should—"

Patrick clamped his hand over Jasper's mouth and gave him a stern glare.

"Trust me. This isn't the cave. Now, grab this rope and hang over the side. I'll pull you up when he's gone. Just don't make a splash."

CHAPTER 9

WHERE IS JASPER CHUN?

With a sigh, Jasper let himself over the side of the *Lady Elisabeth*. Patrick held on to Jasper's hands until he slipped silently into the river. After that Patrick straightened up and strolled into the salon.

"He is gone, I tell you!" Mr. Li did not look happy as he faced Mrs. McWaid. "I hold you responsible for actions of your son and for kidnap of my worker!"

"But, sir," Mrs. McWaid tried to settle the man down while Patrick's father tied up the rowboat on the opposite deck. "Everything's going to be all right. The boys are back. You have nothing to worry about."

"What's that you say, Sarah?" Mr. McWaid looked puzzled as he pulled himself up on deck. "The boys are back?"

She nodded, and Mr. McWaid finally noticed Patrick, standing in the far doorway of the salon.

"Goodness, Patrick, where have you been?"

Considering what had just happened in front of the warehouse and who was aboard the *Lady E* with them, Patrick could understand why he looked a bit upset.

"He's fine, John." Mrs. McWaid moved to hold her husband's arm. "I already got the full story. It wasn't his fault."

"Then whose fault *was* it, now? You'll tell me that? We had a close call a few minutes ago, and now I have to go right back to the warehouse before those fellows return again. But Mr. Li is still concerned about Jasper Chun being missing this morning."

Patrick gulped and backed away. His father was sweating and looking as if he wasn't in the mood for small talk.

"Jasper Chun!" Mr. Li pronounced his sentence as if he were a judge, pounding his right fist in his left palm. He bellowed at Patrick, "YOU know where he is! YOU are responsible!"

"Now, wait here, Mr. Li." Patrick's mother sprang to his defense. "At least let the boy explain. Let's not go jumping to conclusions."

"The only jumping I see is Jasper Chun—jumping away from Mr. Li." He thumped his chest. "My worker. Where is he?"

Patrick cleared his throat and shook his head. "He's not your property."

"Patrick." Mrs. McWaid stepped up and put her arm around her son. "You must be respectful when you talk to Mr. Li."

Patrick nodded. "He's not your property, *sir*, and you cannot take what rightfully belongs to him."

"Son!" said Mrs. McWaid, but Mr. Li put up his hand to repeat his question.

"Jasper rightfully belongs to *me*! He is *my* worker, so where is he? You know!"

"Maybe he has to work for you," countered Patrick. "But he's not *yours*."

"Bah!" Mr. Li stomped his foot and started looking under tables and behind chairs. "Let me tell you about this runaway. I pick him off the street, give him a second chance in life. How does he repay? He lies all the time. And he steals valuable statue from temple in China."

"That's not true!" interrupted Patrick, but Mr. Li ignored him.

"When I found out, I took statue back for temple. But it was lost in ocean. Now the boy, he lies to you, too. He lies about *everything*."

Patrick thought for a moment about what Jasper had told him. Lies? He couldn't imagine how it could be so. And yet, there *was* something odd about Jasper. Becky had noticed it, hadn't she?

Am I the only one who hasn't caught on? Could Jasper really be lying to me?

"Sarah." Mr. McWaid looked at his wife. "What's gotten into Patrick? Is Jasper on board or isn't he?"

Mrs. McWaid looked at Patrick, then at Mr. Li, who was pushing in the door to the captain's state-room, searching every corner of the boat. She started to say something, then bit her lip.

"John, it's not right."

"No, it's not right, the way he treats Jasper." Patrick's father eyed Mr. Li as he made his way around the paddle steamer. "But it's not the only thing 'not right' around here. Three vigilantes nearly shoot their way into the warehouse over there by the wharf. I understand their concern, but it's not right, what they're trying to do. And now it appears a legally indentured servant is escaping. Well, I don't think that's right, either. Is it?"

"John . . ."

"What does 'indentured' mean, Pa?" Michael wanted to know. "And what's a 'vigilante'?"

Patrick started to explain, "I think it means—"

"Not now, children," his mother cut him off.

"Patrick, you tell me the truth—now." Mr. McWaid looked Patrick straight in the eye. "Is this Jasper Chun fellow on the *Lady Elisabeth* or isn't he?"

Patrick held his breath. Mr. Li was searching the deck now, just above the place where Patrick had lowered Jasper into the river. He even tripped over the rope strung across the deck—the same one Jasper was hanging on. But Mr. Li only mumbled and kept up his search.

Don't make a noise, Jasper, thought Patrick, but he could not avoid his father's stern gaze. Mr. Li continued his search up to the wheelhouse.

"I can't lie to you, Pa."

"You've got that absolutely correct, young man. Now—"

"He is not here!" puffed Mr. Li, swinging back down from the wheelhouse. "Must be hiding on shore. Or maybe he run to Ballarat."

Again the Chinese man approached Patrick, but Patrick looked at the deck and was suddenly very busy, pretending to take care of some chores.

"It is your fault, McWaid," said Mr. Li, wagging his finger again. He didn't give Patrick's father a chance to speak. "You are responsible for actions of your wild son and for missing servant Jasper Chun. If I do not find him soon, *you* will pay."

"Now, wait a minute, Mr. Li," objected Patrick's father. "You know I was just trying to help."

Mr. Li shrugged. "I get boy back, or you pay me. In fact, since there is no more gold rush, maybe that is good. Either way, does not matter to me how I get my money. Now, back to Goolwa wharf."

Mr. Li snapped his fingers and lowered himself into the Mc-Waids' rowboat.

Mr. McWaid whispered a question for his wife. "How did we get ourselves in the middle of all this?"

He also had a stern word for Patrick. "We'll talk when I get back, young man."

Patrick knew they would.

"You tell Jasper Chun he cannot get away!" shouted Mr. Li as Patrick's father rowed him back to shore. "You tell him, I find him. And when I do, he will be sorry. Very sorry!"

Patrick didn't answer, of course, but kept his eye on Mr. Li. The man reached the wharf, climbed back up, and continued on his way as Mr. McWaid hurried back.

Good thing those fellows on horses aren't still there, thought Patrick. He watched his father row back to the *Lady Elisabeth* and climb aboard; then he heard a *thunk* on the far side of the paddle steamer. Jasper was still in the water!

"Sorry! I'm coming!" Patrick slipped over to the far side of the *Lady Elisabeth*, out of view of the wharf, and bent over the side of the boat. Jasper was still there, all right, but Patrick almost panicked when the other boy looked up.

"Are you all right?" asked Patrick, not waiting for an answer. By the pale look on Jasper's face, he was afraid to know. Jasper managed to shake his head.

"Give me your hand," cried Patrick.

The others crowded around as Patrick struggled to pull Jasper aboard.

"What in the world?" sputtered Mr. McWaid. "I expected something was going on, but not this."

"It was my fault, dear," said Mrs. McWaid. "But that Mr. Li— I'm just not sure we can trust him."

"I don't know as we have a choice in the matter," replied Mr. McWaid matter-of-factly. "Still, I can't believe you stood here and didn't tell Mr. Li the whole story."

"I'm sorry, but . . ." Mrs. McWaid didn't seem to know how to finish. Instead, she ran to fetch Jasper some dry blankets.

"Up here, young man." Patrick's father reached down a strong hand to help Jasper up.

Jasper shivered as he dripped all over the deck. His teeth were chattering, and his arms were covered with goose bumps.

"Is it really that cold?" asked Patrick. "You seemed all right before Mr. Li came on the boat."

With the sun on their shoulders, it felt quite warm to Patrick, but Jasper's shaking made it seem downright freezing.

"All of a s-s-sudden . . ." Jasper tried to explain how he felt, but he could not.

"Here, you don't need to explain." Mrs. McWaid hurried up with an armload of threadbare gray blankets. "Let's get your clothes off and you dried off."

Patrick still kept an eye on the shore, but he couldn't see Mr. Li anywhere.

"N-no," Jasper raised his voice, and he held his stomach before crumbling to the deck with a groan.

"There, come on." Mrs. McWaid put her arm around him, as a mother would do. "We'll just wrap this blanket around you, and you can change into some of Michael's dry things."

"I . . . I am . . . all right." But Jasper could only shake his head and pull his knees to his chest as he shivered and groaned.

Patrick reached down to help the boy, and his hand brushed against Jasper's forehead. He could feel the heat, and he clamped his hand on the boy's forehead in alarm.

"Ma!" cried Patrick. "He's shivering, but he's burning up, too!"

Mrs. McWaid nodded with wide-eyed alarm when she checked the boy's forehead herself.

"Patrick's right, John. He *is* burning with fever. We need to get him to bed."

"All right." Mr. McWaid frowned and nodded. "Patrick, you take him into the state-room. We'll keep him here tonight if we need to."

Patrick helped lift Jasper to his feet and guided him into the salon, down the short hallway, and into the room that used to belong to his grandfather—the captain's state-room. It was the only room on the boat with a real bed, curtains, and a door.

"I sure don't know what hit you so quickly," said Patrick as he set Jasper down on the edge of the bed.

"I d-do not know, either." Jasper couldn't control his shivering. "H-hot and cold."

Patrick nodded. "I've had the influenza before. I know how it feels. Here, I'll help you with that shirt."

"N-no thanks." Jasper shook his head and pushed Patrick away.

"What? Come on. You can hardly move."

But Jasper insisted. As he fell to the floor, he was still pushing Patrick away.

"Get your mother," insisted Jasper. "Please get your mother!"

When Mrs. McWaid emerged from the captain's state-room a short time later, she pushed through the small crowd that waited around the door.

"Well?" asked Patrick and Michael in the same breath. Their father looked nearly as curious as they followed Mrs. McWaid into the galley.

"Is it the yellow fever, like those men said?" asked Michael.

His mother shook her head and dried her hands on a towel. "I can tell you two things. First, Jasper is quite sick. I don't think it's yellow fever, though honestly I couldn't tell you precisely what yellow fever looks like."

"Hmm." Mr. McWaid didn't look pleased to hear that news.

"I think it's the influenza," continued Patrick's mother, "or something like that. In any case, she's going to be resting for a while."

Michael wrinkled up his nose in a question. "What do you mean 'she'?"

"That's the other thing I can tell you. Jasper is an odd name for a girl."

"What?" Patrick couldn't believe what his mother was saying. "That's not possible, Ma. I was with him for hours. He talks like a boy. He says things like a boy. I was in a cave with him, and . . ."

"Are you sure he's a girl?" asked Michael. "How do you—"

Patrick put his hand on Michael's arm, and Mrs. McWaid looked at them with her eyebrows raised.

"Excuse me, my dear son, but I can tell you that Jasper is most definitely a girl."

"Won't Becky be surprised," Michael said. "A girl named Jasper."

"I have a feeling maybe Becky knew." Patrick started back toward the state-room door. "Or at least she knew something wasn't right."

"But why?" Michael still wondered. "Why would Jasper lie to us about something like that?"

Mrs. McWaid shook her head. "You're going to have to ask her yourself. Just don't get too close."

Patrick crossed his arms and was about to march in without knocking, then thought better of it, backed up, and knocked three times on the door. Jasper was wrapped in a cocoon of blankets, still shivering. She didn't look up when Patrick stepped in, and Patrick didn't say anything at first.

"Y-you must think I am horrible," Jasper finally whispered. Patrick was about to snap back that yes, he wasn't too happy about how she had lied to him and everyone else. And who did he think he was—rather, who did she think *she* was—pretending she was a boy all this time? Something like that.

Patrick clenched his fists, trying to find a clever way to make Jasper know what he was thinking.

Jasper, he thought. *If he's a girl, then that's probably not his real name, either.*

"If it h-helps," mumbled Jasper, "I am sorry."

The words cut through Patrick's thoughts of how to make Jasper feel worse than she already was feeling. Patrick took one look at the shivering boy—no, girl—and unclenched his fists.

"It's all right," Patrick found himself saying. Besides, it was hard to stay mad at someone who looked so sick. "But why didn't you tell me before?"

"It . . . it is a long story." Jasper burrowed down under her covers a little more and closed her eyes. I do not know if I can tell you r-right now."

"You don't have to tell me right now. I know you're not well."

"No, wait a minute." She seemed to change her mind. "I *want* to tell you. But you must . . . you have to promise me you will not tell Mr. Li."

Patrick looked at Jasper, and her dark eyes told him she was telling the truth this time. All the truth.

"All right," he agreed. "Only, no more—"

"No more lies, I know." She took a deep breath and stopped shivering long enough to tell her story.

CHAPTER 10

THE PRETENDER

Jasper didn't look at Patrick as she explained. "If Mr. Li learns I am not a boy, he will never let me see my father. I know that for certain."

Patrick frowned. From what he had seen of the man so far, he thought she was probably right.

"You can see why I pretended to be a boy, can't you?" Jasper's eyes pleaded. "It was the only way I could ever see my father again."

"So everything you told me—"

"I wish it was not true, but it is. My only lie was about being a boy."

"Which is a pretty big thing, when you think about it." Patrick tried to keep himself from chuckling, but Jasper smiled along. "But what about your name? Is it really something else? Jasperina?"

Jasper laughed, then held her chest in pain. "No, it is just as I said. The missionary back in China who taught me English was just joking when he gave me that name. It was because I was always playing with the boys. Climbing ladders, running races, that sort of thing."

Patrick studied her with a puzzled expression.

"I used to win most of the races, too," she added proudly.

"And they still called you Jasper?"

"I thought, well, why not? But do you think I look like a boy, really?"

"No, of course you don't!" Patrick replied without thinking; then he realized how funny it sounded, especially after Jasper had fooled them all. "Well, that is, I used to think you did. But now that you mention it, ah, you look . . ."

Patrick didn't know how to finish the sentence. Jasper just shivered more and more.

"Actually, Jasper, you look ill more than anything else." He turned to yell for his mother's help. "Ma? You'd better come here!"

Michael prayed for Jasper that night at dinner, that she would be feeling better by the morning. So did Becky, and her tears watered the plate in front of her. They all prayed as Jasper lay quietly moaning in the bunk that evening, burning ever hotter with the fever, then shivering, then burning again. Finally Mr. McWaid told them they should go to bed.

Patrick couldn't, though—not when he overheard Jefferson talking to Becky out on deck.

"I just can't stay here," Jefferson told her. "There's a job on a steamer bound upriver in a few days, and I aim to be on it."

Becky mumbled something Patrick couldn't understand, and Jefferson lowered his voice, too. Finally Patrick couldn't stand it. He poked his head out the side door into the soft evening air.

"You don't mean it, do you, Jeff?" Patrick's ears tingled. "After all this time with us, you're just leaving? You can't do that."

"I can and I will." Jefferson yanked his canvas sailor's ditty bag shut, breaking the cord. He threw down the string in disgust. "I've been thinking of a change for a long time."

"You have?" The news caught Patrick by surprise. Jefferson had never said anything like that before.

"And besides," Jefferson mumbled, "your Chinese friends can help run the boat."

"I can't believe you're saying that, Jeff." Becky's voice was strained and hoarse. "You're not like that horrible ship captain and his men."

Jefferson dropped his shoulders and sighed. "I didn't mean it that way. I just—"

"Then how *did* you mean it?" Patrick stepped out to stand on deck.

"You want to know what I meant?" Fire shone in Jefferson's eyes, almost enough to push Patrick back into the river. "You really want to know?"

"I . . ." Patrick stammered. Jefferson advanced as if they were in a fight, until Patrick had backed up against the side of the boat.

"Jefferson, please—" Becky whispered, but Jefferson kept coming.

"Well, let me tell you something about my mama." Sweat glistened on Jefferson's brow.

"Whatever you say." Patrick gulped. Jefferson had hardly ever talked about his family. In fact, only once before, that Patrick could remember, and that had been some time ago. His father had been killed during the American Civil War, Patrick knew, or just after. But his mother?

"Mama got sick, you understand?" Jefferson's voice choked up, and he pinned Patrick against the wall. Patrick just stared and nodded lamely, terrified of the red-eyed Jefferson.

"I'm sorry," Patrick squeaked, afraid of saying anything else.

"She got the fever, some kind of fever. I don't know. Even the doctor didn't know for sure. We didn't have any medicines. Nothing. My aunt Charlotte, she tried to give her some roots and tea, but it only made her sicker. So she just lay there in bed with the fever until she died, and we couldn't do anything to save her."

"Jeff," Becky whispered, "you never told us that."

"And she didn't complain a word. She just—" Jefferson put his head down and wept. Patrick rested his hands gently on the older boy's shoulders. What else could he do?

Patrick's parents were now both standing outside, as wide-eyed and surprised as the rest of them. Michael peeked at the scene from between his parents. Mrs. McWaid started to say something, but her husband told her no. Jefferson had started, and he was going to finish. Through his sobs, he was going to finish.

"So I just can't stay here and watch this again. You've been good to me, all of you, and I thank you kindly. But I . . . I just can't be here and see it again, that's all."

"We understand." Mr. McWaid finally cleared his throat. "And you're certainly free to—"

"No, sir," Jeff interrupted, and it was the first time Patrick could ever remember his friend speaking in that tone to their father. But this was not the Jeff he knew.

"No, sir, you don't understand. No disrespect intended, sir, but you *can't* understand."

Mr. McWaid didn't say anything else. Patrick still couldn't believe it. His speech over, Jefferson just picked up his bag and turned away. That was it.

"So go ahead," Patrick blurted out before he knew what he was saying. "You left us once before. Go ahead and do it again!"

Patrick wished he could have pulled the words back as soon as they were out of his mouth.

"Patrick," said Michael. He would of course defend Jefferson. "That's not nice."

Patrick gritted his teeth. *That's not what I meant to say!*

Jefferson stiffened but kept walking. A moment later he slipped off the *Lady Elisabeth* into a waiting boat.

"Jeff . . ." Becky's eyes filled with tears. He stood up in the boat and looked at her.

"I'm sorry." He shook his head. "Maybe I'll see you in Echuca after this fever thing is all over. I hope the girl gets better."

And then he was gone.

"Ma?" Patrick knocked softly on the captain's cabin door but heard nothing. He guessed it was close to midnight—Jefferson had left them only hours before. Patrick knocked again, then slipped inside.

"I thought you should get some rest, Ma," he whispered.

"What?" Mrs. McWaid's head jerked upright. "Oh, I must have dozed off."

"Here." Patrick rested his hand on his mother's shoulder. "I should help. She's my friend."

"So is Jefferson. Don't forget that."

"You mean, so *was* Jefferson. I didn't do such a good job of saying good-bye, did I?"

Mrs. McWaid didn't correct her son, but smiled weakly and stretched. "You'll see him again. He's just scared, like all the others."

They watched Jasper quietly for a few minutes. The girl gasped for each breath, and her face moved with some kind of bad dream, then tightened.

"You help by praying," Mrs. McWaid said. "I'll help by keeping Jasper as comfortable as I can."

"No!" shouted Jasper, but she was still asleep. "I should go, not you! Please!" She switched over to Chinese as her nightmare continued, and she blurted out a flurry of jumbled words. Finally Mrs. McWaid took the girl's hands and held tightly.

"Now, now," she crooned as if trying to calm a baby. She stroked Jasper's black hair. "You mustn't cry out so. You're just dreaming."

Jasper's eyes fluttered open for a moment before she smiled and fell asleep again. Mrs. McWaid went back to dipping the washcloth in her basin and dabbing Jasper's forehead lightly with the cool water.

"Can we catch what she has?" wondered Patrick.

"You go back to bed," Mrs. McWaid commanded without answering the question. "We'll be just fine."

Patrick nodded and backed into the dark hallway. But before he returned to his sleeping mat, he checked out the window. He could still imagine seeing the three men on their horses, threatening his father and the Chinese men—but of course they weren't there. And where was Jefferson? The moon cast long silver shadows over the wharf, and everyone in town seemed to be asleep. For now it was quiet, but Patrick had a sinking feeling that was going to change soon. Very soon.

"John, her fever hasn't broken all night," said Mrs. McWaid. "She needs to see a doctor."

It wasn't because his mother had a loud voice. It was the edge of concern, the near panic that woke Patrick early the next morning. Patrick lay in his bedroll, listening, trying to hear what his parents were saying. A soft pink morning light filtered in through the salon windows above his head.

"You don't understand," answered Mr. McWaid. "With everything that's happened, I don't think—"

"Are you saying the doctor in Goolwa won't help her because she's Chinese?"

"No," Mr. McWaid snapped. "The people here in Goolwa are decent folk. It's those three troublemakers I'm concerned about. If they hear—"

"They already think all the rest of the Chinese are a threat. And look at her. She's burning up."

"All right, Sarah. I'll go see what I can do. Try to keep her as cool as you can."

By the time Mr. McWaid stepped out of the state-room, Patrick had already pulled his clothes on and was lacing up his boots.

"I'd like to go with you," Patrick whispered and stepped over Michael.

Mr. McWaid put his hands on his hips and looked for a moment as if he would say no, but Patrick beat him to it.

"Please?"

"All right. I wouldn't mind the company."

Minutes later father and son hurried through the dusty Goolwa streets, checking shop windows for signs. The dentist. A lawyer. Three shopkeepers. They weren't the first ones awake in the river port. It was barely six-thirty, yet Patrick could hear hammering on a half-built frame house. A delivery man hurried by in his boxy wagon. And off in the distance, Patrick thought he heard a few people shouting. It seemed like a normal waking-up morning.

"Here it is," whispered Mr. McWaid. Patrick looked up to see if there was any life in the loft above the office where they had stopped.

"He lives up there, doesn't he?" wondered Patrick. His father nodded and knocked.

"Hello, Doctor?" Mr. McWaid knocked twice, three times, then hit the door with his fist. A window squeaked open above their heads, and a sleepy-looking man poked his head out into the cool of the morning.

"If you've more people with typhoid fever," announced the doctor, "I'm afraid I don't have any more space in the clinic."

"Typhoid?" Mr. McWaid stared up at the doctor. Patrick didn't know what to say, either. The doctor started to pull back his head.

"But wait! It's our friend Jasper," croaked Patrick. "On our paddle steamer. Couldn't you come look?"

"What's wrong with him?"

"High fever, chills. Headache, I think. He can hardly move."

"He's burning up," added Mr. McWaid.

"Well, so are four sailors, right here in my clinic."

"But how?" asked Patrick.

"My guess is they took on bad water somewhere."

Bad water. For an instant Patrick remembered the water jug that had washed up at Koala Beach, the water he drank. But he felt fine.

"Takes maybe three weeks for a person to get sick from typhoid," continued the doctor. "But you know how deadly it is."

Patrick didn't know for sure, but it sounded serious enough.

"So what do we do?" he asked.

"Go back home. Keep your friend in bed and as cool as you can. Keep everyone away. I'll be there as soon as possible."

"Right, sir. Thanks." Mr. McWaid nodded seriously and turned back, Patrick at his heels. Neither said a word as they threaded their way slowly back through the streets of the waking town.

"You know how deadly it is." The doctor's words echoed in

Patrick's mind, and he walked right through a thick cloud of dust as a shopkeeper shook a rug out his front door. Mr. McWaid stopped.

"What is it, Pa?" Patrick sneezed.

His father turned around, sniffing the air. "Smoke. I smell . . ."

Patrick caught the scent of something burning, too. *Could it be the dust?* They didn't have to wonder long. When they turned the last corner to face the wharf, both Patrick and his father stopped dead in their tracks.

"What in heaven's name do they think they're doing?" whispered Mr. McWaid.

Three men huddled in front of the warehouse, each one holding a flaming torch fanned by the fresh morning breeze.

Not again! thought Patrick. *They're back!*

CHAPTER 11

THEY'RE BACK

"Wait a minute!" Patrick's first reaction was to run at the men with the torches, but his father grabbed him by the collar.

"Hold on, son. Let me go first. You get back to the boat."

"I can't do that, Pa. I can't leave you here alone. You know what these men want."

Mr. McWaid didn't argue. He pulled Patrick behind him as they walked the last few feet toward the group.

"Good day, gentlemen." Patrick's father sounded as if he were out for a morning stroll. "What seems to be the problem here?"

One of the men whirled around, startled at the intruders. When he held his torch high, the flames glittered off his bald head.

"It'd be better for everyone if you stayed away," he said.

"I don't think so." Mr. McWaid crossed his arms and slipped in front of the warehouse's double door. It was closed and barred from the outside. "And I don't think anyone would want the waterfront to go up in flames."

"What, this old building?" The man scoffed but gave Mr. McWaid a little room. "There's no loss. I know the owner."

"Maybe so." Mr. McWaid stood his ground, and Patrick slipped up beside him. "It's the lives inside I was thinking about."

"Don't you tell me about lives!" exploded the man. His face was red with eye-popping anger. "There's an epidemic in this town, and

87

we aim to stop it right here. Even if nobody else has the courage to."

"But it's not the Chinese who are sick!" Patrick put up his hand. He could feel the heat of the torches and the fear on the men's breath. "It's the sailors. That's what the doctor said. The sailors!"

The man hesitated for a moment, as if thinking it over.

"Ah, you don't know what you're talking about, boy. It's Chinese who bring the fever, plain and simple. Now, out of the way."

Patrick was ready to kick the man in the shins, but his father held him back.

"Besides," the man with the sideburns spoke up. "We don't need a fancy doctor to tell us about any fever. He's too busy treating scurvy sailors to help us with the real problem." The man held up his torch and looked to the others for support. His friend with the beard nodded.

"We just came from the doctor," said Patrick. "He's doing all he can."

"Which ain't enough, let me tell you." Mr. Sideburns made a face. "Too little, too late."

"But we must wait until we know more." Mr. McWaid put up his hand.

"You sound just like him," said the bald leader. "Wait, wait. Well, you can just slip down the river in your paddle steamer while we're stuck waiting here with women and children who are dying."

"You don't care about women and children," Patrick blurted out.

"No? I've seen people die on the goldfields after those Chinese come in. I'm not going to let it happen here, and people are going to thank us. Right, boys?"

The others murmured their support.

"You tell them, Gipps!" yelled the bearded third man. Gipps must have been the name of the bald man.

"Now, let's open the door," continued Gipps. "Burn everything inside. These Chinese fellas can find somewhere else to roost."

Gipps opened a jug and splashed kerosene all over the siding of the ramshackle building. "We'll send these Chinese and their fevers back where they came from!"

"Wait!" Patrick tried to think of something else to say but couldn't.

"No more waiting. I'm sorry, but this is how it has to be." Gipps pulled a scarf up over his face; Patrick wasn't sure whether it was for protection from the fever or to hide behind. The man pointed at them with his torch—a burning rag on a stick—and they barely got out of the way.

"You can't do this!" Patrick tried to grab the man, but Gipps jabbed the flames at Patrick like a sword. Patrick heard yelling and someone running toward them. He looked up in time to see Jefferson Pitney sprinting their way.

"Jeff!" yelled Patrick. "What are you—"

"There you are, Pitney," growled Gipps. "We were waiting for you. Thought you were going to come help."

"What?" Patrick didn't understand.

"These are my friends, Mr. Gipps." Jefferson faced the group.

How does Jeff know his name? wondered Patrick.

"Oh, come now," answered Gipps. "You told me last night you wanted to help. So help."

"Jeff?" Patrick tried to look into his friend's eyes, but they were dark and far away. "You're not really mixed up with these men, are you?"

Gipps took a step toward Jefferson and held out his torch, handle first. "Take it," he ordered. "We'll give you the honor."

Jeff looked uncertainly at the torch, held out his hand slowly, and gripped the handle.

"Jefferson!" barked Mr. McWaid. "You know there are people in there. Even if they get out, this is *not* the best way to help."

"I'm sorry, Mr. McWaid." Jefferson set his jaw and took a step closer.

Patrick backed slowly toward the warehouse, trying not to attract any attention. Behind his back, Patrick felt for the beam that held the big doors shut. The men inside hadn't made a sound, but it would be up to Patrick to free them.

"You know right from wrong, Jeff," continued Mr. McWaid. "This is wrong. Dead—"

"Don't listen to him," interrupted Gipps, stepping aside to let Jefferson come forward. "This is for the good of the town. When I met you last night on the street, I knew you were a man of action."

Even while he was talking, though, Gipps gave a wink of a signal to the others. Patrick was the only one who noticed, but they lowered their torches and touched off the kerosene. At the same time Jefferson heaved the flaming torch as far as he could away from the warehouse.

"Nooo!" yelled Jefferson, and Mr. McWaid broke away to put his arm around Jefferson's shoulder. Jeff wouldn't let him, though, and turned away.

"What's wrong, boy?" Gipps taunted him. "Too afraid to do a man's job?"

Flames *whoosh*ed and leaped up the side of the building. Patrick took that moment of confusion to lean back with all his strength and push the beam up and away. One shove, and the door would be open.

"Hey, you!" yelled Gipps, grabbing Patrick by the arm. "Back away from there, I say!"

"You leave him alone!" yelled Jefferson, launching into Gipps with a headfirst tackle. The three of them crashed into the door, suddenly in flames, and it collapsed to the ground.

The entire side of the warehouse was in flames almost before Patrick felt himself shoved through the splintering wood. His father was there, too, trying to pull him free. And what about all the men inside?

"Run!" Patrick yelled into the shadows, but Gipps's two helpers were now dancing through the warehouse, spreading kerosene all over.

"Patrick, are you all right?" Mr. McWaid dragged Patrick back out to the street, a safe distance away.

"I'm not hurt. But what about—"

"There's no one inside," answered his father, holding up his hand to the heat. "I didn't see anyone."

"Are you sure?"

His father nodded, and Patrick could imagine they had probably found a loose board and escaped through the back. Gipps raised his voice.

"The Chinese must've heard us coming and jumped into the river," he told his men as he finally tossed his torch aside. "Saves us the trouble of having to run 'em out of town."

"What happened to Jefferson?" Patrick asked his father quietly. They both looked around, but there was no sign of their friend.

"Must have disappeared into the crowd." Mr. McWaid nodded at the knot of people who had gathered around to watch the warehouse go up in flames. Gipps stood up proudly in front of the group for a speech.

"This is what we have to do to protect our good city," he crowed. "See? You take action. Plain and simple. No Chinese, no fever."

But that's not true! thought Patrick. Even so, he wasn't ready to take on the bald man again. At least not yet.

"But who's going to pay for all this?" wondered an older fellow. He jumped backward with the rest of the crowd as the old roof collapsed in a rain of orange sparks. The sides of the warehouse folded in like a house of cards.

"Let's go." Mr. McWaid frowned as they finally turned away from the smoking warehouse a half hour later and stepped back toward the wharf. No one had tried to put out the fire; they'd just let it burn. "There's nothing more we can do here."

Patrick nodded and kicked a pebble as hard as he could into the river. *We didn't do anything,* he thought, *nothing except waste time. The doctor wouldn't help us, Gipps chased Jasper's people out of town . . .*

"Say, come to think of it," Patrick brightened up for a minute. "Maybe that means old Mr. Li is gone, too. That wouldn't be so bad, would it?"

Mr. McWaid didn't answer and just stood with his hands on his hips at the water's edge.

"What's the matter, Pa?" Patrick stepped up to see. His father pointed at the place their rowboat had been tied up, and then Patrick saw it, too. Three boats, jammed to overflowing with Chinese men, were slowly moving away from the shore. Mr. Li held the commanding spot, at the stern of the lead boat, like a general leading his troops.

"I'd yell at 'em to come back," said Mr. McWaid, looking quickly back at the town, "but I don't think that would be a good idea. Perhaps it's best they keep going."

"But where were they just a few minutes ago?" wondered Patrick.

"Must've been hiding under the wharf, in the boats. Ours included. Then they came out when the fellas up there left."

Then they both realized where the small boats were headed.

"I can't believe it," said Patrick, pointing at the *Lady Elisabeth*. "She's out of bed."

There was Jasper, standing next to Firestorm, waving at the others to join her on the boat.

"I don't understand." Patrick stared at the boats. "She must know Mr. Li is with them."

Way overloaded, one of the small boats was inches from flooding with water. At least they didn't have far to go.

"Come on." Patrick's father scanned the waterfront for another way to get out to his paddle steamer. "We need to get out there."

Patrick nodded and jumped down to a log float, where an old man was dragging a grain sack out of a shed.

"Say!" Patrick helped the man with his load. They dropped it in the bottom of his brightly painted small boat. "If you're on your way out, could you take my father and me to our paddle steamer?"

"Hop in." The man pointed to his boat. Patrick's father stepped aboard as they pushed off once again.

"Sorry, don't mean to trouble you." Mr. McWaid studied what was happening around the *Lady Elisabeth* as they drew closer.

"No problem a-t'all," replied the man at the oars. He had his back turned to the river and hadn't yet noticed the three boats filled with Chinese men. "Everybody's neighbors here on the Murray. Have to stick together, especially when there's trouble. Which boat?"

"The *Lady Elisabeth*." Patrick pointed. The man kept rowing and nodded.

"What trouble are you talking about?" Mr. McWaid asked their boatman.

"You didn't see the fire?" The man paused on his oars. "That bunch of Chinese brought the fever with 'em. A bad case, I hear. First they were all locked in a warehouse, but I hear Gipps and his friends are chasing 'em out of town."

"Oh, really?" Mr. McWaid didn't take his eyes off the *Lady E*. Most of the Chinese had made it to the deck of the paddle steamer. Firestorm was barking his hellos.

Don't turn around now. Patrick closed his eyes and nodded, hoping his panic wouldn't show.

"Say, you don't look too good yourself." The boatman looked straight into Patrick's face, then backed away. They were only a few boat lengths away from the paddle steamer, and gliding closer all the time. "You sure you haven't caught something?"

"Oh, I'm fine, sir." Patrick held his breath and waited to see what would happen when the boatman finally turned around. Along with Firestorm's barking, he could hear the chatter of the men now, and it didn't sound at all like English. Finally the boatman wrinkled his forehead and glanced over his shoulder, then nearly tipped his boat as he whirled around for a better look.

"Man alive!" he whistled through his teeth, then dug in his oars to stop the boat. "You've got the whole bloomin' paddle steamer filled with fever-carryin' Chinamen! And you want me to take you *there*?"

All the men on the *Lady Elisabeth* had turned to see what was happening.

"I'm sorry, friend. . . ." Patrick's father tried to explain, but it was too late.

"I see what's happening here," cried the boatman. "And you're not gettin' me anywhere near that mob. If you ask me, you're daft yourselves! Crazy! Now, get off my boat. Now!"

"Of course. If you just let us off, we'll be on our way," Mr. McWaid tried once more in a calmer voice. After all, they were only twenty feet from the *Lady E.*

"Not another inch!" The boatman was red in the face, steam nearly shooting from his ears. "How do I know the vapors can't reach me out here? Out, out, out!"

Patrick dodged the oar as the boatman swung at them, but his father wasn't as lucky.

"There's no need of that—" The oar hit Mr. McWaid in the stomach and knocked him backward over the sack of grain. Patrick reached out to help his father, but they both tumbled into the water.

"You lunatics can't get away with this!" screamed the boatman. As Patrick and his father paddled the few feet to the waiting *Lady Elisabeth*, the man churned the water furiously with his oars to get back to the wharf.

CHAPTER 12

WONG-HING

"It appears we have some guests," said Mr. McWaid as he climbed out of the water.

Patrick was already standing on deck, looking around at the strange scene. The company of twenty-five Chinese men filled the decks of the *Lady Elisabeth* from bow to stern. Mr. Li immediately set up court in a chair on the far rear deck. He was going to be in control, no matter what, though he didn't speak a word to any of the McWaids.

Some of the men had simple ragbags of belongings, whatever they had been able to drag with them from the wreck of the sailing ship. One held a pot of glowing embers, which he obviously intended to cook over, and still another held a squawking chicken by the legs. He was smiling. Patrick had no idea where the man had found the chicken. And they were all talking excitedly, keeping an eye on the boatman who hurried back to the wharf.

"No, boy." Patrick held Firestorm back from getting too close to the flapping wings of the chicken. Michael was jumping up and down inside the salon, looking out through the windows, while Becky tried to hold him down the same way Patrick held his dog.

"Oh, John, I'm glad you're here." Mrs. McWaid found her husband and gave him a quick hug. "Jasper says they have nowhere else to go. She was trying to help them get aboard, but I made her get back to bed."

"That's good." Patrick's father took the towel his wife offered him. "Let's keep her there."

"So what do we do, Pa?" asked Becky.

Patrick knew that none of the Chinese men could understand more than a few basic words of English. "Yes." "No." "Gold." That sort of thing. So it must have been the way Becky asked the question that made everyone stop what they were doing and look to Mr. McWaid for his answer. Even the chicken stopped squawking.

"Well . . ." Mr. McWaid pulled on his chin as he thought. "First thing we're going to do is feed these people. Then we'll see."

Firestorm barked and broke loose from Patrick's grip, heading straight for the chicken. Feathers flew everywhere in the free-for-all that followed, and somehow the bird escaped.

"Stop the chicken!" cried Michael, running through the crowd. He didn't help matters any, though, and Firestorm was determined to capture a future meal. But with three or four Chinese men in the race, along with Patrick, Michael, Firestorm, and of course the chicken, it was anyone's guess who was chasing whom. Patrick lunged at one of the animals but only came up with a man's leg.

"Hold it!" The chicken flew into his face. But it wasn't over until Becky stepped in. She darted to the front of the race and cornered the chicken on the upper deck, by the wheelhouse.

"There you are, you little hen," she cooed, slipping her hand under the bird's legs like a steel trap. With a smile she presented her struggling catch back to its owner, who smiled and bowed.

"Chay-chay," said the man. He was probably about their father's age, maybe a bit younger, and he had a broad smile.

"You're welcome," replied Becky, bowing in return.

"Did you know what he said?" asked Michael.

"Of course." Becky grinned. "It must mean 'thank you.' What else?"

"She is right" came a weak voice from the main deck below.

"Jasper! What are you doing up?" Patrick looked down to see their friend leaning for support against the wall of the salon, looking up at them with a grin. But even though Jasper was smiling, her face was pale and her cheeks hollow. "Ma said she put you back in bed."

"I had to see what all the excitement was about." Jasper tried to grin as she looked around at all the people, but soon she started shaking again. That's when Mr. Li finally noticed she was there, and he stared at her.

"Boy Jasper!" he cried. "You were here hiding all the time. I knew it!"

"Jasper is very sick"—Mrs. McWaid poked her head outside— "and is not to get up until I say so."

Jasper tried to move, but whatever strength she had must have left her just then. She collapsed in a heap on the deck.

"Oh dear!" cried Mrs. McWaid, rushing to Jasper's side. "I told you to stay in bed. You're not well yet. Not well at all."

Mr. Li scowled but could do nothing.

"I am sorry," whispered Jasper, and her voice was barely above a whisper. "I thought I was feeling better. Perhaps not."

This time there was plenty of help for moving Jasper back to her bed. One man took her legs, another her arms, and they dragged her back inside as the others watched.

"They still don't know she's a girl," Patrick whispered to his sister.

"And they're not going to." Becky gave him a firm reminder with her eyes. "Right?"

Patrick nodded.

Michael spent most of the afternoon guarding his pet koala, Christopher, trying to explain to their new guests in sign language that he was not raising the animal to eat it. But what could he do besides hold the animal up next to him and point to himself? The three Chinese men who were most interested were willing to repeat the word "bear" over and over, loud enough so everyone on the boat could hear it. But Michael needed help, and Patrick watched from the deck as his young brother went to knock on the state-room door.

"Please leave Jasper alone, Michael," Mrs. McWaid scolded him. "She needs to rest. You know that."

"I know. But, Ma, I need to find out how to tell these fellows that Christopher is my pet. And I don't want to talk to Mr. Li."

A few minutes later he scurried back to his koala's box, where the men were still gathered to watch the sleepy animal eat a few eucalyptus leaves.

"Hong," repeated Michael. "It's my hong. My pet bear. HONG!"

The men on the deck laughed at Michael's pronunciation of the Chinese word.

Meanwhile, Patrick and Becky helped with fishing hooks.

"All right," announced Patrick, "my friend told me that back in Arkansas he used to fry river catfish in a skillet with a little butter, salt and pepper, and . . . you don't understand a word I'm saying, do you?"

A young Chinese boy smiled and nodded at him as they baited hooks for their fishing lines. He was about Jefferson's age, fifteen or sixteen, and he would answer back in Chinese for everything they told him in English.

"Well, he understands what we're up to." Patrick speared on a hook another worm from the can of bait Jefferson and Becky had brought back from Goolwa before Jeff had left. It was coming in handy.

"That's for sure," agreed Becky. Patrick liked how she didn't seem to mind baiting hooks with the rest of them. She held up a worm for the others to see.

"Worm?" she asked the Chinese boy.

"Wong-hing!" he replied, holding up his own worm. "Wong-hing."

"Well, how about that," declared Patrick. "We now know all we need to know in Chinese. We can say the word for 'worm.' "

"Well, all the wong-hings are in the water," replied Becky. "Now we just wait for the fish to start biting." She turned again to the boy who was helping them, put her palms together, and imitated a swimming fish with her hands.

"Fish?" she asked. "Fish?"

"Yey." The boy chuckled and imitated her hand motions. "Yey."

Becky tried to repeat the Chinese word, but it didn't come out quite the way it should have.

"Your face looks funny when you try to say those words!" Michael giggled, and Becky joined him. The other boys laughed until the fishing lines started to wiggle in the afternoon breeze.

"We've got one over here!" yelled Michael, jumping to his feet. "We've got yey!"

That evening Patrick did his best to force down one more bite of fish. People on the river said Murray cod was some of the best eating fish anywhere, and he had no reason to argue the claim. But by the end of dinner, it was obvious they wouldn't finish all the cod they'd caught that afternoon.

"Oh, but it was good." Patrick smiled.

"And it saved the chicken's life," added Michael, licking his fingers. "At least for one more day."

"I'm not sure that was such a good thing," replied Mrs. McWaid. She had done her best to help serve the Chinese men, though they seemed to have their own ideas about eating. Many preferred to cook their own food. Mr. Li had his cooked for him and brought to him separately.

"I don't know, either," agreed Becky. "This place is turning into a floating zoo."

"What do you mean?" Michael didn't think so. "There's just Christopher, Firestorm, and the chicken. We don't have a name for the chicken yet. Do you think—"

"You don't put a name to something you're going to have for supper the next day," interrupted Patrick.

"That sounds like something Jefferson would say." Michael let

Firestorm lick his tin plate, but only when his mother wasn't looking. "I miss Jefferson."

"Maybe Pa will see him in town," Patrick suggested. "If he
hasn't left yet."

No one answered. Most of the Chinese men relaxed on the deck
in groups of two or three, watching the sun go down, swatting mos-
quitoes, and finishing their fish dinner. Mr. Li pointed out fish
bones in his meal and insisted that one of his helpers pick them
out.

One of the men at the very front of the boat played soft, flowing
notes on a Chinese flute. Patrick wondered how the man had managed to save the instrument from the shipwreck.

Becky smiled. "The music flows like the river."

Patrick nodded and watched the wharf for signs of his father
returning from his meeting with the town's magistrate. But two
hours had passed, and he still wasn't back. Patrick wasn't sure if
that was good or bad. He noticed his mother looking the same way,
and they sat quietly for another half hour.

"He'll be along," Becky told her mother. A moment later they
heard angry voices coming from the wharf. The flute stopped.

CHAPTER 13

TYPHOID BOAT

"Here he comes," announced Becky. They watched as Mr. McWaid jumped into his rowboat and hurried back to the *Lady Elisabeth*.

"Want some supper, Pa?" asked Michael when Mr. McWaid climbed aboard. "There's plenty of fish left."

"Maybe later, Michael." Mr. McWaid waved off his youngest son. Lines of concern showed clearly on his face as he joined them.

"What's wrong, John?" asked Mrs. McWaid, holding a frying pan still full of fish fillets.

"Ahh, it's that Gipps fella stirring up trouble again. I tried to talk sense into 'em after they burned the warehouse down, but it's no use. And now he's talking to the doctor and the assistant police magistrate—the judge—at the same time."

"Isn't that what you wanted?" asked Becky.

"That's what I wanted, true, but now he's just building up the hysteria. The real magistrate's out of town."

"And?" Mrs. McWaid wondered.

"The doctor thinks it's typhoid fever, Sarah."

Mrs. McWaid gasped and raised a hand to her mouth. Patrick thought she would fall over backward.

"But Jasper," she gasped. "Jasper only has a touch of the influenza, does she not?"

101

"The doctor in town isn't sure, but he doesn't think so. Most of the sailors are sick. One's died already."

"Oh dear. This *is* serious." Mrs. McWaid's face turned even more pale.

Together they watched as a small group of men met at the wharf. A few carried lanterns, but they seemed to be less of a mob and more of an army. One of the men with a lantern waved for the rest to follow in their boats.

"What are they doing?" wondered Patrick. The Chinese men stopped their chatting and joking to watch, too, as the boats drew closer, then stopped. Soon a small flotilla of ten or twelve boats had gathered, each one carrying one or two lanterns. They bobbed like fireflies in a circle around the paddle steamer, and Mr. McWaid turned his head to tell them what was going on.

"That's the assistant magistrate," he whispered to Mrs. McWaid. "The short one with the deep voice. Seems a decent sort, but he really doesn't know what he's doing."

"Where's the *real* magistrate?" asked Patrick.

"That's just it. The actual judge is in Adelaide. Won't be back for months. This fellow is just filling in. And look who's whispering in his ear."

Patrick recognized Mr. Gipps. It was hard to miss the man.

"You there in the *Lady Elisabeth*!" shouted the magistrate. "Are you aboard, Mr. McWaid?"

Patrick's father crossed his arms and stepped up to the railing to face the men, then raised his voice. "I'm here, gentlemen."

"Then it is my duty to inform you . . . ahem . . ." The magistrate unfolded a wrinkled piece of paper and stood up in the boat. Mr. Gipps held on to his belt from behind to keep him from falling over into the water. "Where was I . . . ?"

The magistrate bent over briefly, and Gipps pointed at something on his notes. The magistrate straightened his glasses and began reading. " 'Assembled this day of March 15, 1869, be it resolved that in order to preserve the public health, this special order of quarantine be hereby enacted.' "

Quarantine. Even the word sounded serious.

" 'The vessel *Lady Elisabeth* is to remain anchored at her present location for a period of no less than twenty days and shall during this time not allow passengers on or off in any manner or under any circumstances. Violations shall not be tolerated. Any bodies of the deceased shall remain on board for the entire duration, until such time as the health officials, in consultation with medical authorities, shall deem the typhoid epidemic is concluded and there is no longer a threat to public health and safety.' "

Typhoid! thought Patrick. *Bodies!*

"What's that man saying?" Michael began to cry. "Are we going to die?"

"Of course not, dear." Mrs. McWaid put her arm around Michael and patted his head. "We just have to make sure no one gets sick."

But the magistrate wasn't done. Gipps whispered something else in his ear as the man folded up his official statement.

"Oh yes," he boomed. "There is something else. 'Owing to the . . . er . . . unusual nature of your passengers, we will be placing specially appointed deputies both on shore and on nearby paddle steamers to guarantee that no one leaves prematurely. Signed by special order of the deputy magistrate, William Morris.' Ahem . . . that's me."

"He says we're going to keep an eye on you!" hollered one of the men in the other boats.

"Yes, well." The magistrate cleared his throat again. "Can you make sure your passengers all understand?"

"We'll make certain of it," replied Mr. McWaid. "But what about the doctor? What does he say?"

The magistrate looked confused and whispered something to Gipps.

"Gipps says," began the magistrate. "I mean, *I* say that the doctor is too busy to deal with this matter. It's *my* decision."

"But Jasper is sick!" added Michael, loudly enough that everyone could hear.

"Eh? What's the boy say?" The magistrate leaned closer and put his hand to his ear. "Someone's sick, is that right?"

"The boy," replied Patrick's father. "Jasper. He's in bed, but he'll be up and about in no time. Everyone else is fine."

"We'll see about that. In the meantime, you'll fly this flag."

Someone in the boat wrapped a yellow quarantine flag around a block of wood, then flung it overhand to them. It landed with a *thump* on the deck, sending the Chinese men scurrying.

"No one leaves!" shouted the magistrate with his finger in the air. His boat was turned around, and the flotilla returned to shore. One boat was left behind, however—the one that would keep the first watch on them.

"It's not so bad," Becky said to Patrick just over two weeks later. Day sixteen of the quarantine, to be exact—as Becky recorded it in her diary. Patrick had looked over her shoulder. Tuesday, March 30. That afternoon she had claimed her usual spot in the wheelhouse and was rereading a dog-eared copy of *Robinson Crusoe*. Jasper dozed in the sun just outside the door; she sat on the wide step at the head of the ladder leading to the deck below. Patrick stared out the windows at the unchanging view of the town.

Not so bad? Patrick supposed it could be worse. The yellow quarantine flag still fluttered overhead on a pole they had rigged up. It did a pretty good job of warning other ships to stay away. It was hard to miss. No one even came close.

"Must be your bad breath," Michael had teased Patrick once, before Patrick chased him around the deck. But it wasn't so funny anymore.

Two or three boats still surrounded them on every side, always at a respectful distance, with watchful guards who took turns making sure no one left the *Lady Elisabeth*. A guard even sat at the Goolwa wharf, but after sixteen days, he seemed to be playing more cards with his friends than guarding.

"Maybe *you* don't think it's so bad, Becky." Patrick yawned. "But I can't imagine why they don't just go home. No one is sick anymore. Jasper is fine."

"Jasper nearly died," Becky corrected him. "Or did you forget that she was shaking in bed for nearly a week?"

"I didn't forget." Patrick stopped picking on his thumbnail and looked over at their friend. "But it wasn't the typhoid fever, or we'd all be sick, too."

"Typhoid takes a few weeks to make someone sick. You don't know what it was for certain."

"I know that, Dr. Becky. I was just talking about Jasper."

"And I was just talking about the rest of us."

"All right, you two!" Jasper finally opened her eyes, and from her expression she looked as if she had a headache. "I know I am still a guest on this boat, but do you think you could stop arguing for just a day or two?"

Patrick looked back out the window. "Sorry. I'm glad you're feeling better. We're all just tired of sitting here."

"Speak for yourself," put in Becky. She sat up straighter. "I'm enjoying my book, if you don't mind."

"I *don't* mind, but I sure can't understand why you'd want to read *Robinson Crusoe* over and over. What is it, the third time?"

"Only the second time," she replied, not taking her eyes from the page. "And if you had some other books I could read, I wish you'd tell me."

"I have never read *Robinson Crusoe*," Jasper tried again to break up the bickering. "But you find new things the second time through, right?"

"Like this." Becky nodded and put her finger on a page. "Do you remember, Patrick, the part where he was shipwrecked on the island, all alone and very sick, and he found the Bible in the sea chest he had from the wrecked ship?"

"I don't remember that part." Patrick had read the book only once, and that had been a couple of years ago. "I can never remember books after I've read them."

Becky nodded. "I know. You read too fast."

"I do not. Just faster than you do."

"No, that's not the point. The point is—"

"All right, all right!" Jasper put up her hands.

"I'm sorry . . . for my brother." Becky smiled. "As I was saying before I was so rudely interrupted . . ."

Patrick made a face at his sister.

"I was saying that when Robinson discovered this Bible, the first words he turned to were from the Psalms: 'Call upon me in the day of trouble: I will deliver thee, and thou shalt glorify me.' "

"Psalm 50." Jasper closed her eyes and smiled. "Verse 15."

"How did you know that?" Patrick couldn't remember Bible verses quite that well. "Are you sure?"

"Maybe you should look it up." Jasper shrugged her slender shoulders, as if it were no great feat. "You have a Bible, don't you?"

Patrick felt the gentle jab. She knew they had a Bible. He just hadn't been reading it much lately. Remembering didn't make him feel better. In fact, now that he thought about it, he didn't feel all that good. His head . . .

"No fair," he argued. "Now it's two girls against one boy."

Becky glared at him.

"Sorry, I didn't mean to bring that up." He looked around to see if anyone had heard the part about "two girls." No one was close; most of the Chinese men were up forward just then.

"But you know, Jasper," Patrick continued, "people are going to find out about you someday. We can't keep it a family secret forever."

"I do not care about keeping it a secret forever." Jasper stood up slowly and tugged at her braid. "Just long enough so I can get to my father."

"Well, we're not helping you very much," he told her. "Not by sitting here."

"It is not your fault." As she had done a dozen times before, Jasper went over and picked her ivory treasure out of its hiding place behind the river charts. Carefully she held it up to the sun. As always, it seemed to glitter and come alive. The statue made Patrick smile and worry at the same time.

"Someone's going to steal that thing," he told Jasper. "Especially if you keep showing it off."

"Don't worry." Jasper carefully replaced the ivory koala in a cloth sack Mrs. McWaid had sewn for her. A string around the opening was long enough to hang the sack around Jasper's neck if she wanted. "No one is ever going to see it."

Patrick supposed she was right, but he sighed and stared out the window to check on Mr. Li. It had become almost a game, seeing how the man kept track of them every day. Only it wasn't very fun.

"I wish it would cool down," he told the others, wiping the sweat off his forehead. "It's getting so hot."

Jasper looked at Becky and pulled up a sweater around her shoulders. "Is he joking?"

"I don't know." Becky shrugged.

Patrick shivered and wiped the sweat from his forehead. He wasn't sure, but when he looked down at the deck below, Mr. Li turned his head quickly and stepped away.

CHAPTER 14

MIDNIGHT GOOD-BYE

Patrick was already awake that night when he heard the scuffling noise of someone walking. For hours he had been half awake, tossing and turning, dreaming of fire. His head throbbed in pain, and his pillow was soaked with sweat.

I've got to get a drink, he told himself, throwing his sheet to the side.

But just getting up was a lot harder than he had imagined.

"Whoa!" he whispered, swaying and grabbing for anything to keep his balance. "Feels like we're in a storm."

Patrick stumbled toward the kitchen, sure that he would wake up everyone else.

"I feel horrible," he mumbled, groping in the dark for a tin cup. He knew his mother kept a water bottle up on the shelf, but he couldn't quite find it in the dark. And then he heard a breath of surprise from behind him.

"Who is there?" whispered Jasper. Patrick nearly let the cup slip out of his fingers as he whirled around. He froze when it hit the floor with a clank and waited to see if anyone else woke. Becky turned in her bed.

"Oh, it's you." He heaved a sigh of relief when he saw the moonlight reflecting off Jasper's face. Around her neck she wore the sack that held her statue. "But what are you doing up?"

"I should ask you the same question." Jasper looked puzzled.

"Just getting a drink of water." Patrick poured himself a glass. "Want some?"

"No. I am leaving."

"Leaving?" Patrick squinted at her face for a clue. "Why?"

"The quarantine is almost over. No one else is sick. . . ."

Except me, thought Patrick, shivering and sweating at the same time.

"So you're just leaving? Just like Jefferson? At least he said good-bye."

"I left a note to thank you. But I am the reason Jefferson left. I am ashamed."

"It's not your fault you were sick." Patrick knew there was something else, and he paused before going on. "What about all that you said about how you owed Mr. Li? How you promised to work for him?"

Jasper swallowed hard. "I did. And I will. I will pay him back everything I owe. Just not now. I must find my father first. Then . . ."

Patrick took small breaths, trying not to shiver in the cool of the evening. He held his head.

"Are you feeling all right?" whispered Jasper.

Patrick shook his head. "I . . . I'm not sure. Not too good, maybe."

"Maybe you will have to stay in bed for a while like I did." When Jasper smiled, the moonlight flashed on her white teeth. "Perhaps I will see you again."

"Wait a minute." Patrick frowned. "You're not going to shore by yourself. They still have guards out there for the quarantine."

"I did not forget. I was going to swim."

"You can't swim without me," Patrick blurted out before he remembered how he felt. But then it was too late. "I'm coming with you. At least to the shore."

"But you would be in danger—"

"Not at all. Now, let's go before I change my mind."

Jasper didn't argue. She hugged the cloth sack to her chest and turned toward the door. Patrick mopped his forehead again, straightened his shoulders, and followed her out onto the deck.

I'm crazy for doing this, he told himself, *especially the way I'm feeling. But she's even more crazy. Better to keep her from getting hurt.*

They stepped carefully over a couple of snoring Chinese men. Patrick froze in midstep, afraid his chattering teeth would give them away. He tried not to breathe, but his head was spinning.

"Are you coming?" Jasper motioned to him with her hand. He grabbed a handrail for support, afraid of collapsing right there.

"I'm right behind you," he whispered. He nodded back at her and pointed toward the rowboat bobbing next to the *Lady Elisabeth* in the dim moonlight. Actually, there were two: One of the boats the Chinese men had borrowed from the shore had still not been reclaimed. But it was obviously leaky and half full of water.

"Rowing will make too much noise," he whispered to Jasper. "Get in the water and we'll push that boat to shore."

Otherwise I'll sink to the bottom of the river, he thought, *the way I feel right now.*

His head still throbbed, and the back of his neck felt as if it had been hit with a club. Maybe the water would feel good after all.

And my legs are noodles, he decided, falling to his knees at the edge of the boat.

"Quiet," said Jasper, and she took his hand as he flopped into the water between the two boats. "We do not want to wake up the dog."

"Sorry," replied Patrick, but he was afraid it was too late. A moment later he heard the *click-click* of Firestorm's claws on the deck and a happy yelp as his pet launched himself into the rowboat for a ride. The dog greeted them with a *woof* and his usual licks to their hands and faces.

"Ohh," Jasper groaned softly. "I was afraid of that. But we will make more noise trying to get him back up on deck."

"Right." Patrick was ready to agree to anything. But where were the guards who were supposed to keep them from coming and going? Weren't they watching? He looked toward one of the guard boats, but all he could make out was a dark shape. He saw no lights, no lanterns, no one moving.

"You . . . be . . . quiet!" Jasper whispered as she pointed her finger sternly at Firestorm. He licked the finger and wagged his tail. Patrick felt the boat moving toward shore as they kicked silently.

Or actually, as *Jasper* kicked. Patrick just gripped the side of the rowboat as if his life depended on it and drifted along as best he could. Firestorm seemed to enjoy the ride, sniffing for night smells with his quivering nose. Patrick smelled them, too—the damp grass on shore, the mud, the water itself.

"That dog . . ." murmured Jasper. Firestorm wagged his tail eagerly and jumped from one side of the boat to the other, sloshing the water back and forth.

"Do you see where we're going?" wondered Patrick as they drifted with the lazy current past the dark shapes of anchored paddle steamers. From behind the rowboat, he could see nothing. Suddenly they bumped into a wooden hull.

"What. . . ?" Jasper peeked above their rowboat hiding place. Firestorm scurried about the boat, whimpering.

"Quiet!" Patrick warned his dog, though he knew it was no use. They bumped and scraped down the side of the larger boat, even as Jasper tried to pull them away. But she ducked back down when a dim pool of light flickered overhead.

"Eh? What's this?" came a groggy voice from above. A long shadow of a man projected out over the still river. Patrick held on with his fingernails and ducked everything but his nose and mouth under the water.

"Well, how about that?" boomed the voice from above. "You out cruisin' the river, mate?"

Patrick could see Firestorm's tail wagging over the edge of the boat. He had found a new friend.

"Say, you're that mutt with the two-colored eyes." Patrick wasn't sure of the riverman's voice, but at least he sounded friendly. "Jake, look here, it's the dog from the *Lady E*. Just drifted over in a rowboat."

"Sure he did," answered another man, sounding much crankier.

"And he probably steers the paddle steamer during the day, eh?"

The man laughed. "Come on, boy. We'll take care of you till we can get you back to your home."

"Quit talking to the dog and go back to sleep!" complained the other man. "It's four in the morning!"

"Relax, mate."

Patrick heard the man talking more to the dog. He must have picked up Firestorm and tied up the boat, then disappeared back to where he was sleeping. Patrick and Jasper waited quietly, trying not to make breathing or splashing noises. Patrick hoped his constant shivering wouldn't make a sound.

"Is he gone?" whispered Patrick after Jasper had checked over the top of the boat. Jasper nodded.

"Let's go." Jasper reached up, untied the boat, and pushed off.

This time Patrick looked over his shoulder to make sure the man on the paddle steamer didn't see them drift away. The light was out, so he couldn't tell. But Firestorm padded out to the edge of the deck, wagging his tail. He barked once, then twice.

Hush! Patrick wanted to say, but he couldn't. *You'll be fine.* Jasper kept kicking, and finally they drifted far enough away so they could no longer see the dog. Patrick thought he heard a squeaking sound.

"Do you hear that?" asked Jasper.

They stopped, and so did the sound.

"Thought I heard someone rowing," said Jasper.

"I don't hear anything," whispered Patrick. "Let's keep going."

The next bump they felt would be the Goolwa wharf. And this time it was as dark and quiet as they had hoped for, with only the soft *swoosh* of the river lapping at the round pilings. Another guard would be there, but he wouldn't be marching back and forth.

He'll be asleep, wished Patrick as they pulled up underneath the wharf.

Patrick tried to forget about his shaking and aching as they pulled the boat up to shore, but he couldn't.

"You should get back to the *Lady Elisabeth*," Jasper told him. "I do not know why you came with me. You are sick."

Patrick could not argue with her. He would have said something back had he not heard steps on the wharf.

"He is up there," whispered Jasper, pointing over their heads. The guard. It had to be. So what was the dark shadow that came up silently behind Jasper, from behind a piling? A sudden sliver of lantern light hit them in the face.

"Well, well," hissed a voice, and it sounded more like a snake than a man. "Jasper Chun."

The words told Patrick everything he did not want to know. How had Mr. Li followed them?

CHAPTER 15

HIDE AND SEEK

"Get away from here, Patrick!" Jasper wiggled and squirmed, but it was not enough to escape Mr. Li's iron grip. The man squeezed her from behind. Patrick stood his ground, unsure what he should do.

"Ah, yesss," said Mr. Li, a serpent in the darkness. "Go run, Mister Patrick. It is not *you* I want, only Jasper Chun. And he is trying to escape."

"You are evil!" Jasper finally replied. "Why did you follow us?"

"Why?" He chuckled. "Boy Jasper worth money. Good English money. And you are my property, just like statue."

"What?" Jasper still struggled, and Patrick jumped into the fight. But the man was surprisingly strong. Too strong. He used Jasper like a shield.

"Don't pretend." Mr. Li shoved Patrick away, sending him sprawling on his back in the mud. "I see you with statue back on the boat. But it belongs to me, remember? Give me the bag."

Mr. Li must have reached for the statue just then, as Jasper put up a mighty struggle and kicked him in the shin with the heel of her shoe. He roared as they both tumbled over.

"Patrick!" Jasper pulled the cord off her neck and thrust the sack with the statue toward him. "Take it! Run! I am right behind you."

What else could he do? Patrick's mind wasn't working as it usually did. He was frozen with fear, the fever, or both, and couldn't seem to make up his mind. But he took the statue and ran, forcing his noodle legs to climb up the riverbank to the town above. He wasn't sure if Mr. Li was chasing them. All he could hear was the pounding of his own heart.

Climb! he commanded his legs, and he crawled up the scramble of gravel and dirt next to the wharf. He knew Jasper had to be right on his heels.

Run! He had to tell his legs to move; they would not work by themselves.

Breathe! But every breath was pain and fire. His head felt as if it would explode. And one thing was sure: He would not be able to run far.

"I am right behind you, Patrick!" cried Jasper.

Without looking back, Patrick sprinted down the first street he found. A right and a left and he was already lost. But his legs would hardly move any longer, no matter how he commanded them. He was close to passing out.

"We should have stayed on the *Lady E*," he told Jasper, but it was too late for that. His mind was not working clearly enough to think straight. It was the fever, all right.

"Jasper?" He looked to the side, then listened for a sound to tell him Jasper had followed. A dog barked in the distance. "Jasper, where are you?"

"I am not going to hurt you, boy!" cried Mr. Li, his voice echoing closer with every step. "I just want to talk."

"I don't think so." Patrick wheezed and stumbled. Where could he hide? What had happened to Jasper? Patrick staggered on.

What am I doing? he asked himself. *Is it just for this statue?*

"Wait!" Mr. Li was just around the corner, behind him.

"No," Patrick reminded himself. "It's for Jasper."

There had to be a hiding place somewhere. Behind this crate? Too small. Down this alley? No, it came to a quick dead end. He stood behind a vegetable wagon in back of a store, trying to decide.

There's nowhere else to run, he finally told himself. He climbed up and over the wagon's back gate with a grunt. It took all the rest of his strength, but he didn't let go of the statue as he burrowed in between half-empty baskets of beans and carrots.

Is Mr. Li here yet? Patrick wondered as he showered himself with carrots. He dug his head into the produce until he heard the pounding of footsteps come around the corner. He could barely see what was happening, but he had to look.

"Boy?" yelled Mr. Li. He kicked through a pile of crates stacked up against the back wall of a shop, causing a thunderous racket.

"Come out from where you hide, boy," crooned Mr. Li. Now it sounded as if he were inviting the neighborhood to a birthday party. "You and your friend do not know what you are doing. I just try to help you."

Help us? Right!

A carrot top tickled Patrick's nose, but he held his breath. Mr. Li whirled and pushed over a stack of wooden crates with a swift kick.

Good thing I didn't hide there, thought Patrick.

"Listen, boy. I know you are here. You take something that does not belong to you."

You're right about that.

"And it does not belong to your friend, either. He steals it."

Patrick's muddled mind had a hard time translating the "he" back to "she." Jasper. He was about to blurt out, "No, Jasper is a she," when he realized just in time where he was.

Don't do anything stupid, he told himself, wrestling with his mind for control. He pinched himself to stay awake. But he was fading fast, and he knew it. He should get help. Who would help him? He gripped the statue through the cloth sack.

It's all your fault, you little koala. If it wasn't for you . . .

Patrick was almost ready to throw the koala out into the alley when Mr. Li took another swipe at a garbage crate.

"See here, boy. Here is good money for you. Come out now, and I give you a share."

A share? Patrick's tortured mind spun. *A share of what?*

A dog howled from behind him in the dead-end alley. Mr. Li

117

turned and headed straight for the vegetable wagon.

Here he comes. . . .

A window opened above their heads.

"Quiet down there!" shrieked a woman from the window. She followed her complaint with a pan full of potato peelings, which hit Mr. Li right on the top of the head.

"Wait!" began Mr. Li, but he could do nothing except shield himself.

"I say, there's enough troublemakers in this town without one more," complained the woman. "Honestly, waking up the entire neighborhood."

Mr. Li just grumbled and turned on his heel. Actually, whether he said anything else or not, Patrick wasn't sure. He could remember no more as he surrendered to the fever.

Patrick never knew exactly how long he lay crumpled in the back of the vegetable wagon. An hour? No, maybe two or three. Long enough for the sky to turn pink, but not long enough for everyone to have woken up. But *some* people were awake, and they laughed as they walked past the wagon. Was it a dream?

They'd better be quiet, thought Patrick, *or that woman will dump her potato peels again*. But he couldn't remember if what had happened was real or a dream. He had never felt quite like this before. His head was still locked in a hammering fog, and he shivered. The next thing he knew, he was lumbering down the side of the street, following three men like a wandering shadow.

Where am I going? Patrick wondered, but he never really woke up. Still he heard the voices ahead, and something in the voices sounded familiar. *What are they saying?*

"This will prove that we know how to take care of our own," said one of the men as they turned the corner. His bald head led the way. "No Chinese will ever dare to come back."

Patrick just blundered after them, watching them file into an inn.

They're . . . they're talking about the quarantine, Patrick told himself, and he knew, even in his fever, that he should find out more. But they were inside, and he was outside. He waited, trying to decide what to do.

Should I follow them?

Patrick was about to step out of the shadow of a door well when he recognized Mr. Li coming down the street toward him, walking briskly, looking as if he were trying to find an address. He stopped in front of a corner building, paused, and came closer.

This is even worse! Patrick couldn't go back now. He pulled open the door and stumbled inside, hoping he wouldn't have to face anyone.

He didn't dare look straight at the three men, but they didn't look up from their table. It was set in a sparse front parlor decorated only with stiff wooden chairs, a couple of tables, and paintings of horse races on the dirty yellow wall. If he could just slip by into a hallway . . .

"Say, how about getting us something to eat, boy?" drawled one of the men. "We're the only ones here."

"Yessir." Patrick kept his back turned and hurried around a corner to safety. They never saw his face. And he certainly didn't turn back to see who else had just walked in and let the door slam. He knew. In the silence he could almost hear the jaws drop.

"Who are *you*?" asked the bald-headed man, Mr. Gipps. "Aren't you still quarantined?"

"My name is Li. I was told I find you gentlemen here."

A chair scraped against the floor.

"Sit back down," said Mr. Li. "I am not sick."

"That's not what we heard," said one of the other men, and Patrick was fairly sure it was the man with the sideburns. "We heard there were more Chinese dying out there on that boat."

Mr. Li laughed quietly. "You should not believe everything you hear."

Patrick quietly opened a broom closet and slipped inside.

"All right." It was Mr. Gipps again. "Just stand where we can see you. Don't get any closer."

119

"As you wish."

"Li, did you say?" Mr. Gipps was asking the questions. "Aren't you the one who paid for the—"

"I pay ship passage for the group, yes. But now there is no gold to pay me back."

"That's a good one." The third man chuckled. "Mr. Li lost all his money. Now you need a loan, is that it?"

"No. I think there is way I can help you."

The chuckling stopped. Patrick wished he could see what was going on. Mr. Gipps asked more questions.

"*You* . . . think you can help *us*?" said Gipps.

"Allow me to explain."

The men lowered their voices, and Patrick pressed his ear to the closet door. Mr. Li sounded as smooth as ever.

"But for me to do this," continued Mr. Li, "I need . . . money to help with . . . deport cost."

"Yeh, sure, Li. Deportation. Throwing them out of the country. You mean you want money to sell out your own people, right?"

"That is crude way of saying it, Mr. Gipps," retorted Mr. Li. "This is all business proposition. I am businessman. How could I know gold rush was over when I brought them here?"

"You could have asked."

"Things change," continued Mr. Li. "Now you do not want these people here. We help each other. Agree?"

"You talk as if you're not one of them! We're just trying to protect our town."

"As I say, I can help you."

Patrick struggled to understand what was going on, wondering how Mr. Li could say such things about the people he was supposed to be taking care of. A damp mop tipped off the wall and fell on his head.

"Did you hear that?" asked one of the men.

CHAPTER 16

CALL UPON ME

Patrick held his breath, afraid the men would get up from the table and discover his broom closet hiding place. He didn't dare move the mop that had just clattered onto his head.

"Ah, must be the boy cooking our breakfast," answered man number three. "Say, lad, we're getting hungry out here."

Patrick didn't dare answer. The men continued talking in low voices.

"I don't see why we need you," said Mr. Sideburns, "when we can just—"

"Do not be foolish," interrupted Mr. Li. "You cannot just go out there and . . . put them on ship back to China. You need my help to move them to right place. Or else they just run away."

"So that's where you're going to help us?"

"They do anything I say." Mr. Li sounded sure of himself.

"All right," said Gipps. "So it's three days to the end of the quarantine. You're saying you can deliver them all to us by Saturday night?"

"Trust me."

"That's just it. I *don't* trust you, Mr. Li. In fact, you're disgusting. But if you deliver them to us, we'll do the rest. No one will be hurt. *Then* you'll get your money."

Patrick couldn't see anything, but he heard a chair scrape

across the wood floor. The meeting was over.

"Dusk Saturday." Mr. Li sounded farther away.

"Oh, and Li—"

"Yes?"

"Stay out of sight until then, will you?" Mr. Gipps sounded tired. "In fact, I'm going to show you a place where you can stay out of the way. . . ."

The door to the street squeaked open and slammed shut. Mr. Li was gone with Gipps.

"Whew! Think Gipps's plan will work? He knows we can't give this Li character any money!"

"Ah, but the Chinaman doesn't know that," replied Mr. Sideburns. "And not only are we *not* going to give him any money, but he's going to be out there when it blows."

Out there? Patrick tried to imagine what that could mean. It seemed so obvious, but he just couldn't make his mind work.

"Blows?" The other man didn't seem to understand any better than Patrick did.

Mr. Sideburns laughed. "Listen. Gipps is too cautious. You stay with me, and we'll take care of this problem my way. We'll send them away, all right, but not the way Gipps thinks."

"But what about the paddle-steamer captain?" asked the other man.

Mr. Sideburns scoffed. "He's a fool. We'll take care of him, too."

So that was it. The men's dirty deal was done, and the innkeeper finally showed up. Patrick could tell by the clinking of glasses.

"The lad was going to bring us a breakfast," said Mr. Sideburns. "What's taking so long?"

"The lad?" The innkeeper sounded puzzled. "I've no lad working for me. Perhaps you mean my daughter, but I don't think—"

"It was a lad, I say." Mr. Sideburns sounded irritated.

"The *girl* will bring you something to eat right away, sir."

Patrick heard the innkeeper's quick footsteps walking by the closet.

"Can't tell the difference between a lad and a lass," mumbled the innkeeper as he hurried by the broom closet. The two men out in the dining room continued their serious talk.

"So we'll see some fireworks Saturday night?" asked the third man as soon as they were alone again.

"That's what I said."

"Are you sure it's the best way? What'll Gipps say?"

"He'll thank us," replied Mr. Sideburns. "It's the only way."

Patrick waited in the closet for them to finish.

I can't believe this is happening, he thought. *I have to tell Pa*.

Patrick hung to the faint hope that Jasper had gone for help, and he wondered what had happened to her. But he could only stay in the closet. After a while he tried to pray, but his mind only turned circles and stopped at dead ends. The only thing he could remember to say to God was Jasper's psalm.

"Call upon me in the day of trouble . . ." The words drifted into his mind. *". . . I will deliver thee, and thou shalt glorify me."*

I'm calling, Patrick prayed silently, but that was as far as he got. He knew this was his day of trouble. A nightmare that wouldn't end. But he could only doze in the closet. And wait.

Was it safe to leave yet? Patrick had repeated the words of the psalm over and over, not realizing the room had grown quiet. He was about to crack open the door when he heard a woman humming and a splash on the plank floor.

I'd better find my way out of here, Patrick decided.

But he didn't get the chance. Before he had finished the thought, the closet door was pulled open and he lost his balance.

"Ayeee!" The chambermaid let out a scream as Patrick tumbled out onto the floor. Patrick could only stare up at the girl. She held her long gray skirts up with one hand and a dripping bucket in the other.

"Sorry to startle you," muttered Patrick, struggling to his feet. The mop fell out of the closet, and he picked it up to present to her. "Were you looking for this?"

She took the mop without a word. Her wide eyes said everything.

"Well, I'd best be getting along." But when Patrick tried to step toward the door, his feet failed him. He slipped on the slick floorboards, turned an ungraceful spin with his hands beating the air, and wobbled out the door to the street.

The next few blocks were a blur. He thought he knew his way back to the wharf, but he wasn't sure his legs would carry him there.

Goolwa isn't that big of a town to get lost in, he told himself, but it didn't do any good. He even stopped to ask a woman for directions, but she just looked at him the same way the chambermaid looked at him back at the inn.

After that, nothing looked familiar anymore, and the streets all blended into one. How many alleys were there in this town? Maybe he was just walking in circles.

Worse yet, all the men on the street started looking like Mr. Gipps. As Patrick's fever and confusion grew even more, he hid in the shadows, muttering to himself. Somewhere deep inside, he knew his mind was playing tricks on him, but he couldn't stop it.

"I'll have to hide again," he told himself, sighting one more suspicious-looking man. How long had he been running and hiding? Hours? Days? He had to get away from the men.

Hide!

Passing an alley, he found the perfect hiding place. The vegetable wagon again.

The last thing Patrick remembered as he fell asleep was how hard Jasper's koala statue felt, poking him in the chest. He hadn't thought of it for hours, but there it was—hanging in its cloth bag around his neck.

Jasper, he thought, *I wish you'd come and get it.*

Oh! When Patrick opened his eyes, he wasn't sure where he was or what day it was. He was hardly sure who he was. All he knew was that he was terribly sick and that he had just bumped his head on something very hard. A wood floor, perhaps, only the floor seemed to be moving.

And then there was something soft, as well, covering his face. And it smelled—

A melon. A very ripe melon. He blinked open his eyes and reached up his hand to wipe off the smashed seeds. That's when he remembered.

I'm in a fruit-and-vegetable cart, he told himself, trying to sit up. He could not.

His arms and legs felt like lead weights, and he could barely lift his head. The sun beat down on him where he lay wedged and hidden between baskets of carrots and potatoes.

"Jasper," he groaned, "help me!" But the voice that came out of his mouth scared him into silence. It was hoarse and very weak and did not at all remind him of Patrick McWaid's voice. And oh, how the words hurt his throat coming out! He tried to swallow, but his mouth was parched dry. When he tried again, he managed only a whisper. Obviously no one could hear him over the sound of the horses and the grinding wagon wheels. And it wore him out trying.

Anything he did seemed to wear him out. He rolled over on his back and rested for a few minutes. Every bone, every muscle in his body, cried out in pain. He wanted to curl up in a ball and cry, but that would probably hurt even more. So he just lay there, bouncing on a bed of overripe cucumbers as the wagon lurched along. He looked up at the blue, cloudless sky. At least he still had Jasper's statue, tucked in the cloth bag hanging around his neck.

Jasper's beautiful, stupid statue!

It seemed Patrick's right hand had become permanently locked around the ivory bear. And as he gripped the statue, his mind tumbled backward to the nightmare that had brought him there. The escape from Mr. Li. Being sick. Hiding in the vegetable cart. Being more sick. Hiding in the broom closet in the inn. Being oh so sick. Patrick honestly couldn't separate the real from the nightmare. All he knew for sure was that he needed to get back home to the *Lady Elisabeth*.

He wasn't even quite sure just then what he needed to tell his father. But there was something, something very important.

The cart bumped down the dusty road for hours, maybe. Patrick had a hard time telling. His sense of time seemed to run backward, then stop, then race forward and skip.

Forget the time, he finally decided. *I've got to get the driver's attention.*

But how? He was still in the far back of the wagon, wedged between wicker baskets. It was a wonder no one had seen him hiding there. The wagon lurched as it hit a bump.

That didn't feel good. Patrick held on as best he could, but the road only got bumpier. A basket of carrots fell on his head, and like a puppet on a string, Patrick was bumped upright as the wagon hit the biggest bump yet.

Here we go! For a moment Patrick smiled, but he was too slow to hold on. So instead of sitting upright in the back of the wagon, he just slumped forward and rolled right to the edge. He lay there, staring at the dirt road going by before him, wondering what it would take to bump him right off.

Not much, as it turned out. The next jolt sent him flying into the dust. He hit hard, then rolled. He didn't even bother trying to turn his head to see the wagon leave him behind.

I'll just lie here in the sun and dry up, he thought. It didn't seem to matter that he rested his nose in the dirt. Nothing seemed to matter to Patrick anymore.

Would someone else come upon him on the road? *It doesn't matter*.

Would he ever see his parents and Becky again? *It doesn't matter*.

And what about Jasper? *It doesn't matter*.

But it does matter, a tiny voice still argued. And then he heard his sister's voice, as if she were standing on the road right next to him, speaking Jasper's psalm.

" 'Call upon me in the day of trouble: I will deliver thee, and thou shalt glorify me.' "

"Becky?" Patrick lifted his head out of the dust, looking for his sister. He knew it couldn't be her, but what did he really know anymore?

CHAPTER 17

NIGHTMARE ON HIS KNEES

It was not Becky reading the Bible verse, and of course Becky wasn't on the dusty, deserted road beside him. No one was. But Patrick still couldn't shake the feeling that he had heard a very real voice.

"I'm imagining things. I must be." Patrick shook with fright at what he had become. Slowly he rose up on all fours and looked down the road.

"I'm not waiting for the birds to come take me away," he croaked. Even though it hurt like a hundred sore throats to speak, he forced the words out of his mouth. Maybe by speaking out loud, he could prove to himself that he was still alive—that he was not going crazy.

"Do you hear that?" Patrick's voice burst into a loud whisper. "I'm not going to just lie here!"

But whom was he speaking to? *Let the bush opossums hear. Or the wallabies.*

He couldn't spend the energy to care. There was no one to hear him on the road.

And so he began his journey. He knew the road would somehow get him home. He would figure out the why, the how, the when later. Right now it was enough to have the road to crawl on and a goal ahead of him.

A place to go, no matter how far away it was.

Patrick would get there crawling. Forget the fever that hammered his head and turned his thoughts silly. Forget the ache that still cursed his body and made him want to fall down and die.

Now he crawled, one knee in front of the other. Jasper's statue dragged along in the dirt, still swinging from around Patrick's neck.

It must have taken an hour to crawl a hundred feet. Maybe longer. But that's when he made the discovery.

"Footprints!" He looked around to see where they came from.

At first he couldn't find the feet that matched. He couldn't hear the sounds of any people, either. But when he took a deep breath, a warm memory filled his lungs.

Bread baking!

Patrick knew he couldn't trust his senses just then. So he kept crawling, wondering how he had smelled something so wonderful here on such a lonely stretch of road.

He tried to focus his eyes, as they were starting to play the same trick his nose had played on him a moment before. A young boy up the road skipped in Patrick's direction.

"Say, there!" Patrick breathed at the boy, who was spinning a wooden hoop down the road with a stick. The boy skidded to a stop.

"Michael!" Patrick could only see his brother's face on the boy. "You've got to help me, Michael!"

The boy stopped his hoop and squinted at Patrick. He was dressed in near rags, and his hair was wild like a bird's nest. And he couldn't have been more than five or six years old. Younger than Michael.

"Why are you calling me Michael?" asked the little boy. "My name is James. And why are you crawling like a baby? You're too big to crawl."

Patrick nodded but kept crawling. He was afraid that if he stopped, he would never be able to start again.

"I'm sorry . . . James. I—"

"Why are you whispering?" James asked, leaning closer. "I can hardly hear you."

Patrick put all of his strength into making his words loud enough for James to hear. "I need . . . help. Where are . . . your parents?"

"Mother and Father?" The boy's eyes lit up. "Father's out cutting wood. I'll get Mother for you."

James turned around like a top and launched his hoop again. Patrick watched it down the road until it was too blurry for him to see. Had it been real?

Minutes later Patrick had pretty much decided that the boy was a dream. Just like the wonderful smells of baking bread. And everything else that had happened to him since he left the *Lady Elisabeth* with Jasper. Dreams, all of it. And Patrick figured the large woman hollering and running down the road toward him was a very loud dream.

"James!" she screamed. "You get your father right now!"

"I *told* you he was real." James disappeared through a thicket, apparently to get his father.

Patrick kept his head down, feeling more like a dog than a boy.

"Oh my!" The woman stopped at his side and crouched down to look Patrick in the eye. "Where did you come from, boy?"

Patrick slowed but didn't stop.

Dreams can be dangerous, he reminded himself, and he shaded his face with his free hand. *Even if they talk and wear aprons*.

"No one's going to hurt you. Do you understand?"

The woman put her hand on Patrick's shoulder and looked him in the eye. He came out of his waking dream just enough to see she was round faced, a little on the plump side, and quite pleasant-looking. But the look on her face made Patrick feel like a run-over animal she had just discovered.

"Please." It was all Patrick could make himself say. "Please help me."

James returned with his father, who still carried a broad,

double-bit ax. The man dropped his tool in the bush when he saw Patrick.

"This fellow needs help," said the man. He bent down, scooped Patrick up in his arms, and hurried across a field.

"I don't know where he came from," chirped James, skipping along behind them. "He was just crawling down the road in the dirt like—"

"Hush, now, James," said his mother.

The man half walked, half jogged without speaking to Patrick. He *did* talk to his wife, though, in short sentences like "Get some water boiling," and "Find me some clean towels."

The man lowered Patrick onto a soft mat of straw in a warm, dim barn. It smelled like animals and hay, not at all bad. And the mother hovered over him just as his own mother would have. A few minutes passed before the man returned with a bowl.

"Here you go. You'll feel better if you drink this." Patrick breathed in the wonderful steam when the woman held a spoon to his lips. She spooned something warm and delicious into his mouth. It tasted a lot like his mother's chicken soup. He did his best to swallow, and no one seemed to mind when half of the soup dribbled down his chin.

"Drink," said the woman.

Patrick imagined what a baby bird felt like, taking worms from its mother's beak. He felt more helpless than he had ever felt in his life, and he hated the feeling.

But he couldn't fight it anymore. He couldn't crawl anymore, either; his knees were studded with small bits of gravel. All he could do was shiver and hug his shoulders as James' mother spooned more and more soup into him. That part was good. But he still couldn't stop shivering.

Patrick surrendered once again to the fever that had wrung him out like a damp, twisted towel. He felt his head droop, and he hoped that when he woke up again, it would all prove to be a very bad dream. Except for the soup.

No such luck, thought Patrick the next time he woke. Actually, Patrick wasn't quite awake, just in and out of knowing. Again he had no idea how long he had slept.

For all I know, I could be an adult by now, he thought. Golden morning light filtered in through cracks in the barn siding, holding hay dust in its rays.

He knew he wasn't alone, though; he could hear animals in the barn—hens fussing over their meal, a cow shifting her weight. He liked the sounds but wished he could wake up completely.

A sound like a giggle came from a dark corner of the barn.

"Who's there?" Patrick croaked.

Patrick listened and relaxed when he heard the chickens fussing again in the far side of the barn.

That's what the sound was, he told himself. *Just chickens*.

The fog in his mind began to lift . . . slowly. Things were making sense again. More than that, his stomach rumbled.

"Wouldn't some eggs taste great right now?" he asked himself. Ever so slowly he unfolded his legs and tried to stand. He looked down at his knees and wondered what had happened to tear his pants so badly. In the back of his mind, he remembered something about crawling, but it was more like a bad dream. The chickens squawked and flapped their wings.

"Say there, hens. No need to carry on so." Patrick found his whisper voice as he pulled himself up with his arms. He held on to the side of an empty cow stall for balance before finally letting go. For the first time in days, his legs held him up. Just barely.

"Would you look at that," he whispered to the chickens. "I can walk again."

As far as Patrick could tell, the hen house was attached to the outside of the barn. But as Patrick lurched through the hay, he could tell something was wrong. By the sound of it, something— or someone—was giving the chickens a good chase. He put his hand out to open the door, then changed his mind when he heard scuffling.

"Hello?" croaked Patrick.

CHAPTER 18
TOO LATE!

The red-faced boy burst through the door to the barn, nearly bowling Patrick over backward. James. He held a squirming hen in his hands.

"Oh," whispered Patrick. He backed up slowly and tripped over something on the floor, but caught himself. "You're back."

"We weren't sure if you would be able to talk," said James. "My father thought you were going to die."

"Did I?" asked Patrick. To him it seemed like a reasonable question. He certainly felt as if he had. His throat still burned.

But the boy only laughed, a high-pitched chirp.

"Of course you're alive, silly. But you've been sleeping a terribly long time."

"How long?"

"I'm not sure. A whole day. Longer. A long time. My mother said for me to stay away. She said maybe you could make me sick. Can you?"

"I hope not." Patrick thought about it for the first time. "Not unless you drink the same water Jasper and I drank. But if your mother said for you to stay away, you'd better do what she says."

Patrick had never understood those kinds of things. His father had once told him some fevers could jump from person to person.

Typhoid, though, was usually from bad water, the kind the sailors had brought with them.

"Who's Jasper?" James asked.

"What? Oh, a friend. It's a long story. . . ."

The fog in Patrick's head lifted a little more. Patrick gasped as he glanced down at what had caused him to trip a moment before. Jasper's statue sticking out of its sack!

Suddenly it all came flooding back, the bad dream he had been trapped in for . . . How long had it been?

"That's it!" Patrick practically shouted the words as he picked up the statue.

"What?"

"Don't you see?" Patrick wasn't completely sure how it all fit together just yet. But the fog was gone. Lifted. "The statue. I still have the statue."

"I'd better go."

"After all that running and hiding, I still have the statue." If Patrick could have jumped up and down, he would have. "And I remember now what the men were saying when I was in the closet."

"The closet?" James looked at Patrick as if he were crazy. He dropped the chicken and let it scurry away.

"That's right!" Patrick jabbed at the air to make his point as he put together the pieces of his puzzle. "I don't remember everything they said, but I know that Jasper and his people are in danger. And I've got to get back to Goolwa before it's too late!"

Patrick turned and pushed his stiff legs as fast as they would take him toward the barn's big double doors. He was definitely not raving mad anymore.

"It's sure a relief to have my mind back," Patrick added.

"I'm going to tell my mother."

Patrick looked over his shoulder before he pushed out the barn door. "What day is it?"

"I don't know." James put his hands up. "Could be Saturday, could be Sunday. I think Saturday."

"Saturday!" Patrick couldn't believe it. "That means I've lost three days!"

"Hope you find them," mumbled the boy just as they heard a call from outside.

"Jay-aymes!" It must have been the boy's mother. James flinched.

Patrick hurried out the barn toward the calling voice, toward the farmhouse.

"Don't tell her I was here!" called James. He disappeared through a loose board in the back of the barn.

"I just hope I'm not too late," said Patrick.

"Now, listen, boy." The farmer sat at the head of the table, eating a pile of fried eggs and newly baked bread and washing it down with warm, fresh milk. "It wasn't so long ago that we picked you up for dead on the road."

"I knew he wasn't dead, Father," James piped up. He was balancing on the back of his mother's chair, peering around her shoulder and chewing on a crust of bread. He stayed a safe distance away from Patrick.

Patrick just devoured the meal in front of him. He had never known so much food could fit into an empty stomach. He hoped it stayed there.

"Now you tell us your family's in danger," said the farmer's wife, "and you have to run off down the road to Goolwa?" She shoved another plate of eggs in Patrick's direction and poured him another glass of milk.

"That's a good day's ride from here." The farmer put down his glass and wiped his milk mustache with the sleeve of his shirt.

"Yes, sir." Patrick nodded. "But I must go, and right away. I'll run if I have to."

The farmer's wife gasped. "You'll do no such thing, You *can't*! Why, look at you. You should be resting in bed, not running down the road to Goolwa. Who knows what fever overtook you?"

"You've been very kind." Patrick pushed his chair out and stood up—though he needed to put a hand on the table for balance. The farmer's wife gave her husband a worried look, the same way Patrick's mother would look at his father. Finally the farmer frowned and nodded.

"We have no horse. But I'll saddle up Wilberforce for you."

"Come on, Wilberforce." Patrick tapped his heels against the side of the slow-moving donkey as he headed back down the road to Goolwa. "I can walk faster than this."

Which wasn't quite true; Patrick was glad to be sitting down, even on the back of the rangy animal the farm family had loaned him.

Patrick counted the hours as they sauntered along. It had been a while since the big farm breakfast, and Patrick's stomach was rumbling that it was time to eat again.

"Any more bread?" Patrick asked himself, looking into the cloth lunch sack the farmer's wife had packed. He found only one more generous slice of bread slathered with homemade apple butter. Wilberforce looked back as if asking the same question.

"Nothing for you, fella. Just keep going."

The donkey didn't seem to want to listen to Patrick's advice, though. He stopped at the next interesting patch of grass.

"Come on! Not again." Patrick slapped the reins. Wilberforce ignored him. The donkey looked up when he was finished, flicked his ears as if to say, "I'm in charge here," and slowly put one hoof in front of the other.

Patrick sighed and bounced in the simple leather saddle. "I'm *never* going to get there if you don't hurry up a bit. Look—even the flies are going faster than we are."

Wilberforce didn't care and just plodded on, flicking his ears as he went. Patrick finally gave up and nibbled at his last sandwich, watching the land flattening out ahead, toward the river and Goolwa. He knew the town had to be coming up soon.

Maybe it was the sun overhead, or the buzzing flies, or the steady *ploppa-ploppa* of Wilberforce walking down the dusty road.

But as the donkey continued at his own donkey pace, Patrick must have dozed, even though his mind was swimming with what he had to do. And when he woke he found himself on the hard ground—no longer in the saddle.

"Oh!" Patrick shook his head and rubbed his tailbone as he rose to his knees in the dust. Wilberforce took the chance to hurry ahead. He didn't even turn his donkey head to see what had happened.

"Wait!" Patrick jumped back on his feet. He set off after the animal as fast as he could, which wasn't very fast. "Stop, Wilberforce!"

Serves me right. Patrick could have kicked himself. *Serves me right for sleeping. I'm not much of a donkey rider.*

Wilberforce, up ahead and out of reach, sounded as if he were laughing.

Hee-haw.

"Here, Wilberforce." Patrick whistled, holding out his hand to the animal.

But Wilberforce had his own ideas. From a safe distance he snorted suspiciously at Patrick as he nibbled on a patch of tall dried grass. And as soon as Patrick came within grabbing range, he scurried off with another *hee-haw*, a flick of his tail, and a kick of his hind legs.

"Oh, come on." Patrick tried again and again, but it was the same thing. Once, he nearly had a hand on the animal's reins as they dangled in the dirt. But again and again, Wilberforce made a quick escape.

"No, stop!" Patrick dove for the donkey on his fifth try but only came up with a mouthful of dust. This time he didn't get up. He pounded the dirt with his fist, which he thought would help him feel better. But it only made his hand hurt.

"How am I ever going to catch this animal?" he asked himself. Tears of frustration made the world turn blurry. Then he remembered how much he needed to be in Goolwa. He thought of Jasper and what Mr. Gipps and his friends were planning.

"I remember." And what had been a bad dream cleared even

more with the tears. He remembered hiding in the closet. The mop falling. The men making a deal with Mr. Li, and how they wanted to . . . Well, Patrick wasn't exactly sure what they would do with the Chinese men when they had them, but he was sure it wasn't good. He checked his bag again to make sure he still had the statue.

Good, he thought. *At least the statue is still safe. Not that it matters anymore. Nothing matters if I don't get there in time.*

He felt something else, too: the remains of his squished sandwich, which had turned to a mess of crumbs, rocks, and apple butter.

"Ohh." Patrick picked it out and threw it on the ground in disgust. Yes, he was still hungry. But not *that* hungry. He felt like crying again. A branch snapped behind him.

CHAPTER 19

SET TO BLOW

"Now what?" Patrick looked over his shoulder to see Wilberforce staring at the sandwich, his nose quivering. The donkey must have circled back to get closer to the food.

"Oh, so you're interested in the sandwich, are you?"

Patrick almost fainted from the donkey's bad breath, but he allowed the animal to stretch closer and closer to the ground. Close enough to grab the harness again.

"There you are!" Patrick grabbed Wilberforce before the donkey could snatch up the sticky pile of crumbs. And then he had an idea.

"Maybe I can use this sandwich after all."

Patrick pulled a ragged handkerchief out of his sack and wrapped the sandwich remains loosely inside, then snapped off a long stick from a nearby tree and skewered the donkey meal with the sharp end. Wilberforce was still sniffing.

"Never met an animal who likes apple butter so much. Or maybe it's the bread." Patrick smiled. "Whatever it is, you can come and get it."

Once back in the saddle, Patrick held the stick out as far as he could, but straight in front of Wilberforce's quivering nose. The meal was just out of reach.

"Here we go!" Patrick watched as the donkey hustled to reach the sweet treat—but of course couldn't. Wilberforce kicked up a cloud of dust as they hurried down the road to Goolwa, faster than ever.

"Whoa, that's almost too fast, Wilberforce." Patrick tried to sit up in the saddle, but the constant bumping had worn him down. He was sure blisters would keep him from sitting down comfortably for weeks.

The other bad news was that his arm felt ready to fall off after holding the stick out in front of Wilberforce's face mile after mile. Still, the donkey never seemed to tire of the possibility of getting a treat.

If I ever get off this thing, Patrick promised himself, *I'll never ride another donkey in my life*.

The good news was that Goolwa was just down the road. As the sun set directly behind them, Wilberforce started breathing hard and slowed down.

"Just a little farther, old fella."

This time there was no getting lost. Even the tired donkey seemed to know the way to the wharf. He would follow the main road, past a collection of stone houses and wooden shacks, then past the courthouse and police station, and finally down to the wharf. Not a problem this time.

As he rode into town, Patrick thought seriously for a moment if he should stop at the police station and explain what was going to happen. He thought he saw the magistrate through the dim window, sitting with his back to the street, obviously talking to someone. Mr. Gipps stood up and slammed his hands together, making an angry point. Patrick caught his breath.

"Oh no." Patrick shook his head. "Now I've really got to find Ma and Pa. Before it's too late."

The streets were nearly empty except for the usual after-dinner crowd coming and going in front of the two hotels, the Australasian and the Corio. But it looked as if Goolwa had pretty much gone to bed for the day.

Good thing, thought Patrick, *or we'd be running them over in the street*. Wilberforce wasn't exactly the steering type.

Patrick looked up at the darkening sky and wondered what time it was. As he passed the Corio, his mind went back to what the men had told Mr. Li. On Saturday night, they had said. That's when they wanted the Chinese men. Dusk, after sundown. And then there was the part about the "fireworks." Patrick still wasn't sure what that meant exactly, but he didn't like the sound of it.

"Hurry, Wilberforce." Patrick saw the darkening shadows across the street as his enemies. He had come all this way. Maybe he was already too late. But he wiggled the stick even more as they raced down Cadell Street directly toward the place where the horse-drawn railroad from Victor Harbor met the wharf.

"Excuse me!" he had to yell as a surprised woman scurried for safety. "I'm sorry. He doesn't steer too well."

"Why, I've never—" The woman pulled a shawl tightly around her shoulders as she went on her way. Wilberforce hurried down the street, braying and kicking. Patrick held on for his life as they neared the waterfront, where they nearly plowed into a storage shed at the foot of the wharf.

"That's it, old boy." Patrick finally pulled the stick back enough for the donkey to sink his teeth into the handkerchief, and Wilberforce came to a halt.

We made it!

But now that he was there, Patrick wasn't quite sure what he had expected to see on the wharf. A big scene, maybe. Or the Chinese men being dragged away. Surely Mr. Li or Mr. Gipps, though Patrick had already seen Mr. Gipps at the police station.

Instead, the wharf was quiet. A mangy-looking dog sitting on the end of the wharf scratched at a flea. A lantern came on in one of the paddle steamers tied up nearby. Most of the paddle steamers at the wharf looked empty.

Out on the water, however, the *Lady E* looked like a party boat as she belched black smoke from her twin smokestacks. The decks were covered with happy, waving men, and little fluttering English flags hung crisscross from cords all over the boat. The flags were left over from the time when Prince Alfred, duke of Edinburgh, had visited Australia and ridden the *Lady E*. A dozen lanterns lit the scene. *A party for the end of the quarantine?* wondered Patrick.

"Hoorah," shouted a few of the men in unison, and the voices drifted across the water. "Hoorah, hoorah, hooRAH!"

Someone must have taught them a few English cheers. And it certainly didn't look as if anyone was in danger. Patrick couldn't see Jasper anywhere, though.

Did I imagine everything? he asked himself, looking around once more. *Could I have the day mixed up?*

But he knew he hadn't imagined what had happened to him. And it *was* Saturday dusk.

I'd better get out there.

He slid gratefully off the donkey's back and dropped to the wharf, but the sack around his neck caught on the saddle and slipped off. When Patrick looked down, it clattered to his feet and fell through a crack in the wharf.

"Ohh," Patrick groaned. "All this way, and I lose it here in Goolwa."

He tied up the donkey as best he could and started for a ramp that would lead down to the water. The statue would be all right, just stuck in the mud somewhere.

Noodle knees, he complained to himself. His legs moved, but slowly.

"But I don't see why I have to—" a voice from behind him made Patrick's heart stop. Mr. Li!

Patrick didn't dare stay where he was; he slipped quietly around the corner of a waterfront shed to listen.

"This is not what we agreed," Mr. Li complained loudly, struggling to pull his arms free. The two men on either side of him held tight. Mr. Gipps was still back in the magistrate's office, but here were his two friends!

"Quiet!" replied one of the men, and Patrick remembered the voice. Mr. Sideburns. "Or we'll arrange to place you on the boat, too. Is that what you want?"

Mr. Li didn't reply.

"I didn't think so," continued Mr. Sideburns. "We just want you to see what happens so there won't be any doubt in your mind."

"Barbarians," hissed Mr. Li. "Murderers. All of you."

"People have to make sacrifices sometimes." The other man's voice was flat. "We do what we have to do."

"But Gipps promise they would not be harmed." Mr. Li sounded more desperate than Patrick had ever heard him.

"That's what Gipps wanted to do. But plans change, you know? Old Gipps doesn't know it, but I'm in charge now."

"And the doctor—"

"Hang the doctor. He knows nothing about fever. He's just a lot of talk."

Patrick swallowed hard and did his best to stay standing. His knees wobbled as the man kept up his speech.

"In fact, Gipps is up there talking to the doctor and the magistrate right now with those McWaid folks, talking about ending the quarantine. Talking and talking. Said he'd take an hour or two. Bah." He spit on the ground.

Ma and Pa were in the police station! Patrick could have kicked himself. *And I rode right by!*

"Same as what happened five years ago when my baby daughter died of your Chinese fever. Talking and talking. No action. Well, I'm through talking. Now's our chance. I'm doing this for my little Emma."

"Gipps told me they would just be sent home to China." Mr. Li drew a deep breath. "And so did you. You promise I would be paid. But I will not have their blood on my hands!"

"Too late for that," Mr. Sideburns told him. "People will remember this accident. We'll be rid of the fever for good, and our town will be safer for it. It's for the best."

Mr. Li struggled again, but the two men were too strong.

"But I will tell you this, Li. As long as you keep quiet, we won't hurt *you.* Why do you think I'm letting you stay here while all your other Chinamen are stuck on the paddle steamer?"

"I do not know. . . ." The wind had surely been taken from Mr. Li's sails. "It makes no sense."

"Oh, it makes sense all right, Mr. Li. See, we need you to go home to China and spread the word. You're going to tell everyone to steer clear of Australia."

"And if I do not?"

"Listen, I'm not a violent man. But you don't give me any choice. If you'd rather take a ride out to the paddle steamer, there's still time before the boiler blows up. Maybe a half hour, if we're lucky. What will it be?"

Mr. Li hung his proud head.

"It's going to look like an accident," repeated Mr. Sideburns, and his voice was almost a whisper. "We'll make sure of that. You just keep your mouth shut and watch the fireworks. When it's all over, you'll be on a boat back to China."

Now Patrick understood far too well what they were talking about. Before his grandfather died, he had told them of terrible steam-boiler accidents on the river, accidents that had ripped sturdy paddle steamers to bits. People had been killed. And this was going to be another "accident," unless . . .

Half an hour? Patrick sweated in the shadows, wondering how he could get out to the *Lady Elisabeth* in time to warn everyone, especially when these men were in the way. Were Michael and Becky on board, too?

"I actually feel sorry for the poor devils," continued Mr. Sideburns, "if you can believe that. I don't enjoy this one bit."

"But quarantine is over." Mr. Li wasn't going to give up just yet. "No one is sick."

"How many times do I have to say it?" Mr. Sideburns raised his voice a notch, then quieted back down to an angry whisper. "I don't believe you. I don't believe the magistrate, or the doctor . . . I don't even believe Gipps. We're taking care of this problem *my* way! Not Gipps's way. Not your way. *Mine.*"

Wilberforce chose that time to announce himself with a friendly *hee-haw.*

"What's that thing doing there?" wondered Mr. Sideburns. The donkey shuffled closer, pulling his reins free.

He's probably looking for another sandwich, thought Patrick.

"Just a donkey," said the other man.

"Well, get him out of here." Mr. Sideburns snapped his fingers and quietly directed his bearded friend to step over and push on the donkey while he held on to Mr. Li. "We don't want to call more attention to ourselves than we already have."

Patrick saw his chance—maybe his only chance....

CHAPTER 20

INTO A MILLION SPLINTERS

If I can just slip behind them, Patrick told himself. But a moment later, out in the open, he thought maybe that hadn't been such a good idea. He took another step out from behind the shadow of the shed, where he had been hiding. Two steps, and then he froze.

"Come on, you dumb animal," wheezed the other man.

"Keep it quiet," insisted Mr. Sideburns, looking nervously toward town. Patrick still couldn't see anyone else around.

Exasperated, the bearded man finally hauled back and slapped the donkey across the hind leg. Wilberforce responded with a swift kick that caught the man in the side and spun him around with a gasp.

"Why, you!" he cried.

Wilberforce lost no time trotting away toward town. And Mr. Sideburns chuckled quietly as his friend was left holding his side. "I don't know who's more the dumb animal," he said.

But his grin turned to a frown when he noticed Patrick standing on the wharf.

"You there," said Mr. Sideburns. "What are you doing?"

Patrick shrugged and tried to look as casual as he possibly could. Out for a stroll, maybe. Or fishing. But surely Mr. Sideburns would recognize him.

"Nothing, sir." Patrick's knees knocked together as he searched for something intelligent to say. "That was, uh, my donkey. Always wandering off. I was just out fetching him. My mother's going to be looking for us, too."

"Well, then." Mr. Sideburns dropped his shoulders in relief, apparently satisfied. "You'd better go get him."

Patrick nodded and took a step, but his weak knee decided to fold just then, and he tumbled on his face on the wharf.

Not now! thought Patrick. He rolled onto his side. *Don't let him know how scared you are.*

"Watch out, boy!" cried Mr. Sideburns, hurrying over to Patrick. He traded Mr. Li to the other man. "Are you all right?"

"I'm fine. Just clumsy." Patrick tried to stand, and Mr. Sideburns insisted on helping him up. Patrick did his best to look away as he dusted himself off. But he couldn't escape the glare that followed.

"Wait a minute." Mr. Sideburns took a step back and studied Patrick's face. "You're . . ."

"I'm just leaving." Patrick nodded, and his mouth went dry. "I'm just leaving to get my donkey."

"That's the McWaid boy," warned the other man. He turned to Mr. Li. "Isn't it, Li?"

Patrick backed away slowly as Mr. Sideburns' jaw dropped open for a second, then snapped shut. And Mr. Li still didn't answer. He looked pale and shaken.

He knows. Mr. Sideburns knows.

Patrick knew he couldn't outrun them. He could shout, but the men would be on him in a second. There was no one else in sight to help; all the paddle steamers looked dark except for the *Lady E*, but it was just too far away.

"All right, boy, let's just talk for a moment." Mr. Sideburns had a soft voice when he wanted to sound nice. "Let's talk."

Patrick shook his head slowly and kept backing up as the man advanced with his hand out.

"I'm not going to hurt you," cooed Mr. Sideburns, putting his hand out to stop Patrick. But when Patrick took another step back, his foot hung for a moment in midair, then . . .

"Whoaa!" yelled Patrick, only it didn't come out loud like a yell. He windmilled over the edge of the wharf. Mr. Sideburns managed to lay a hand on Patrick's foot, which flipped him around and helped him to land with a perfect belly flop in the muddy river.

Ohh. Patrick lay still for a moment, stunned by the sting of the river, wondering how something as soft as water could feel so hard when he fell on it the wrong way. He started to sink.

No! he told himself. *Swim!*

Of course, that was much easier to say than to do. At first his arms and legs would not obey. But as the water down deeper began to close in on Patrick, something else took over: raw fear. And even though he knew Mr. Sideburns could be waiting for him on the surface, he wanted even more the air that was waiting there, too.

"Ohh!" Patrick gasped when he finally surfaced. But when he looked up, all was quiet and dark on the wharf. Where was Mr. Sideburns?

I can't worry about that now, he decided, looking across to the lights reflected on the water. Especially not with just a few short minutes before the *Lady Elisabeth* would pop into a million splinters.

I just don't know if I can swim all the way out there. Already Patrick's arms and legs were ready to shut down again, and he wasn't more than ten feet from the wharf.

"Wait!" Mr. Sideburns cried in a hoarse whisper. He had slipped quietly down the plank ramp to where a boat was tied up. Patrick wanted to shout, but he didn't have the breath to spare.

"Swim or drown," he puffed, pushing out farther from the wharf. It was simple, he knew, but it was also impossible. He wished he had a boat there to hang on to, or at least Jasper to remind him about the words to his psalm.

"I will deliver thee," he puffed with each stroke. *"I will deliver thee. . . ."*

"There you are!" An oar dipped into the water inches in front of his nose, a warning from Mr. Sideburns. The man had managed to follow him in a small boat.

"Wait there, now," he said. The man balanced the dripping oar just above the water. "You don't want to go out there, boy. Believe me, you don't."

He still doesn't know if I overheard what they said. Patrick decided to play along.

"Why not? Looks like a party."

But Mr. Sideburns shook his head nervously. "The . . . ah . . . quarantine's still not lifted, you see. Your parents are up at the magistrate's talking it over. No one goes out there just yet."

"But I was out there for weeks," argued Patrick. He decided to hold on to the side of the rowboat for a moment. He had to. "That's where I live."

"Sorry, boy. I can't let you do that. Here, get back into the boat and I'll take you to your parents. How about that?"

Patrick thought for a moment. "Well, the water *is* a little cold."

"That's my boy." Mr. Sideburns smiled and reached out his hand for Patrick to grab. Patrick gathered his strength, gripped the man's hand, and planted his feet against the side of the boat. Then he ducked and tugged as hard as he could.

"Whaaat?" Mr. Sideburns cried as he tumbled over the side of the rowboat. Patrick had caught him completely by surprise. The man bobbed to the surface, sputtering and furious.

"You dirty little larrikin! Why, I'm going to . . . to . . ."

Patrick didn't wait to see what the man could think to do—even though Mr. Sideburns didn't look quite so dangerous when he was in the water. He looked more like a walrus, in fact, paddling and splashing and puffing his cheeks out. Patrick ducked under the boat and came up on the other side.

"You pulled me in on purpose!" called Mr. Sideburns. "I was trying to help you, and you pulled me in!"

Patrick knew what he had to do. He just wasn't sure he had the strength left for it. He reached up for the boat, kicked, and rolled his shoulders over the edge.

Good way to sink the boat, he thought as river water poured in over the top. He nearly slipped backward but gave another kick and tumbled onto the floorboards before the boat righted itself.

"Sorry," Patrick told the struggling Mr. Sideburns, who was

barely holding on with his fingertips to the end of the boat. Patrick plucked the loose oar out of the water, set it in place, and set to rowing.

"Listen, boy," Mr. Sideburns wheezed as Patrick rowed. "I can't swim too well."

There was also no way the big fellow was going to crawl back into the boat as Patrick had. Patrick sighted the *Lady Elisabeth* over his shoulder and pulled.

"Hold on if you want, then," Patrick grunted. "But I'm going out to my paddle steamer."

"No." Mr. Sideburns slipped to one hand. "You're crazy!"

"Maybe. But like you said, I'm just doing what I have to do."

Patrick didn't want to waste his breath talking. He also wished he didn't have to tow the big man behind him.

"I'm not going out there," said Mr. Sideburns. "That's all I'm saying. Turn us around."

"No, sir."

But the man wasn't listening anymore as he dropped off behind the boat. Patrick paused for a moment, worried that he would sink. But as far as Patrick could tell, Mr. Sideburns floated quite well.

How soon? wondered Patrick as he leaned back to row. He couldn't be sure. He expected to hear the explosion any time, feel the wicked little arrows of red-hot shattering boiler hit him in the back.

Don't think about it. As he left Mr. Sideburns behind, he heard the excited shouts of twenty-five Chinese men on board the *Lady E.* That, and Jasper Chun yelling at him.

Jasper?

"Patrick!" shouted Jasper. "You are back!" Obviously she hadn't seen what had just happened on the wharf or in the water. When Patrick looked over his shoulder, Jasper was smiling and waving from the deck of the paddle steamer. Michael was running around from the far deck. So was Firestorm the dog, barking happily at everyone.

Patrick wasn't sure what he was going to do, but it would have to happen fast.

CHAPTER 21

BOILING TEAKETTLE

Bang!

Patrick hit the side of the *Lady Elisabeth* hard, way too hard. But he was in a hurry, and he fell over backward, his legs in the air. Firestorm was the first to jump all over him, showering him with happy licks.

"Firestorm!" Patrick pushed his dog away. "Where did you come from?" But there would be no time for hellos.

"Watch out, Patrick!" Jasper tried to climb down and hold the rowboat away.

"Oh, Patrick!" Michael jumped up and down, as he did when he was excited, and talked as fast as a lightning express train. "We're so glad to see you! Nobody could figure out what happened to you, and we couldn't even get off the boat to look. But the guards brought Firestorm back, and then Jasper came back yesterday and told us that Mr. Li was chasing you. But now the quarantine's nearly over, and Ma and Pa and Becky are up talking to the magistrate. I stayed back to watch Christopher, and nobody else is sick, and you're—"

"No time for that!" Patrick pushed his way past Firestorm and onto the boat. He ran to the engine room, still not sure what he was going to do once he got there. He shook the doorknob in a panic. "Locked!"

"Oh, is it?" asked Jasper, sounding surprised. "Your father sent out a man to look at the engine for us just a few minutes ago. Really big fellow. He said we had a problem refiring and that we shouldn't touch it until he gets back."

"A big fellow?" Patrick held out his hands. "A big man with side-burns?"

Jasper nodded. "Yes, but what—"

"Pa didn't send him." Patrick leaned against the door and pounded it with his shoulder.

"You're going to break it, Patrick." Michael tried to hold him back. "Pa has a key. He'll open it."

Patrick shook his head and wondered what to do.

"What is wrong?" asked Jasper.

Patrick couldn't answer and think at the same time. He picked up a log from the woodpile, pushed past a couple of puzzled Chinese men, and rushed at the door.

Crack! The door shattered but did not open, and Patrick backed up for another try.

"Patrick!" screamed Michael. All the cheering Chinese men cut their hoorahs short and gathered around.

How much time left? Patrick wondered. *Only minutes?* He turned to the others.

"Listen to me," he told them breathlessly. "The engine's rigged to blow up. I can't do anything about it."

"But, Patrick," cried Michael, "the man said—"

"Did you hear me?" Patrick yelled, and it hurt his throat. "Just believe me. You all have to get off the boat now!"

Jasper turned white but repeated Patrick's words to the others in Chinese. Michael rushed to fetch his koala. Firestorm still barked happily, wagging his tail faster than ever. A few of the men gasped at the news, but no one moved. They had been through something like this before, and Patrick thought he understood the look in their faces. The look that said, "Not again!"

"Listen to me, I beg you," said Patrick, turning to his audience. "This isn't a shipwreck. But your lives are in danger. It doesn't look like danger, but it is. You've got to believe me."

The men just stood rooted to the deck, whispering to each other.

"Don't you hear?" Patrick didn't know what else to do, so he ran up to one of the men and pushed him backward off the deck. "Save your lives! Get off, I'm telling you!"

That's when the boiler creaked and popped, and everyone jumped. It might have been just the burning wood or steam escaping from the side of the boiler. Patrick wasn't sure. But he knew there wasn't time to push everyone off one by one.

"It could blow at any minute," he said. "Tell them, Jasper, and get off this boat!"

With that, Patrick rushed at the door once more. With the log as a battering ram, he tumbled through the splintered door and slid on his face into a pile of coal that had spilled on the floor. It was like stepping into an oven. Jasper sprawled in after him.

"I thought I told you to jump!" Patrick stood up, but Jasper came up behind him and grabbed him by the shirt.

"You can't do anything about it, Patrick. You get out of here, too! The rest of the men will follow."

"No!" Patrick stomped his foot stubbornly and tried not to imagine the boat exploding with some of the men still huddled on the deck. Any of the men. So he turned instead to the steam engine. Somehow he would shut it off. Or else . . .

"What do I do?" he cried out, not just to himself, but to God, too.

He stared at the swirling, steaming collection of shining metal tanks, valves, and spinning wheels and held his head in despair. Surely his father or Jefferson would know what to do. But to Patrick, looking at the steam engine was like trying to read Latin. And he had never been able to read Latin. In the meantime, the door to the boiler glowed almost red, and Patrick wiped his sweating brow.

"Have you ever sneezed with your nose plugged?" he yelled at Jasper, searching desperately for a hint—anything to show her how to stop what was going to happen.

"Only once. It made my ears hurt." She looked nervously at the door. "Patrick—"

"I know, I know."

The engine and boiler somehow reminded him of when he was a little boy, playing with his mother's teapot in their kitchen back in Dublin. He'd plugged the spout with a cork just to see what would happen. The cork had blown off and broken a glass, and his mother had given him a good spanking for it.

"That's it!" Patrick knew what to look for. "Something that reminds you of a cork."

Nothing in the tangle of tubes, gears, and levers looked quite like a cork until Jasper pointed to a red handle at the top of the boiler—the part of the engine where the water turned to steam. The part that was ready to blow apart at any time with a mighty explosion.

"There!" Jasper gasped. "Is that it?"

"Sure looks like it."

The red handle was tied off with rope, knotted a dozen times and wedged shut with a crowbar. Patrick wondered how he hadn't seen it to begin with.

But he couldn't quite reach the top, so he took aim with his piece of wood and threw it as hard as he could. And the moment it hit, Patrick realized that might not have been the smartest thing to do. He ducked and put his arms up to shield himself from the deafening hiss.

Jasper screamed.

CHAPTER 22

HE CARES FOR THE RAVEN

Patrick wasn't quite sure if they had stopped the explosion or caused it, but he knew they had to get out quickly.

"Are you all right, Jasper?" he asked as they tumbled out through the shattered engine room door. Jasper didn't answer his question, but her eyes were as big as saucers.

"All right, it doesn't matter," cried Patrick. "Let's go!"

By that time the last three Chinese men on the edge of the deck didn't need any more persuading or pushing. At the sound of the first explosion and the sight of the steam pouring out from behind Patrick and Jasper, they all jumped into the river. Patrick looked up from the river to see the spinning crowbar falling out of the sky, and he watched as it splashed down into the water.

He was afraid to look back at the *Lady Elisabeth*, but almost more afraid to duck his head under the water one more time. He stayed close to Jasper and waited for the final *boom* of destruction that would sink their paddle steamer.

Instead, he heard the boom of his father's voice coming at them from the direction of the wharf.

"Patrick! Michael! We'll be right there."

Patrick couldn't recall a time when his father's voice had sounded better. He looked up to see Mr. and Mrs. McWaid pulling Michael into a boat, just ten or fifteen feet away. Michael gripped a wet bundle under his arm that had to be his frightened pet koala, Christopher. Firestorm was thrashing in the water next to the boat, as well, and Becky hauled him in as if he were a fish in a net.

"Over here, Pa!" Patrick waved wildly, keeping a worried eye on the *Lady E.* Steam and smoke poured out of the paddle steamer's wounded side.

Of course Patrick and Jasper weren't alone in the water. Chinese men bobbed all around them, and some were headed straight back toward the *Lady Elisabeth.*

"Don't go there!" cried Patrick. "It's going to blow up!"

But no one paid any attention. A few of the Chinese men hauled themselves right back up onto the boat. They must have thought the danger had passed. Patrick could do nothing about it, and his voice gave out. He couldn't say "Pa," or "I'm sorry," or anything.

For that matter, he could hardly keep his head above water. His father's boat glided up to them, and Patrick simply held up his arms. Mr. McWaid grabbed him and hauled him out, while Becky and Michael each took one of Jasper's arms and did the same thing. Patrick was dripping wet, of course, but Mrs. McWaid gave him a big hug.

"Oh, Patrick, thank God you're alive," she whispered with tears in her eyes.

Patrick pulled away and shook his head. He opened his mouth, but only squeaks would come out. How could he tell them the boiler in the *Lady Elisabeth* was about to blow up? Or was it?

Another cloud of steam hissed out the side of the paddle steamer. Not an explosion, exactly, but enough to send people scurrying again. A kind of *poof*, and then it was over.

"They plugged it to explode," Patrick managed to whisper into his father's ear. "Mr. Sideburns and the others." Mr. McWaid nodded seriously.

"If they were wanting to sprag the boiler," said Mr. McWaid, "then they didn't do such a good job of plugging it up." He brought them alongside the paddle steamer, and they all climbed aboard. Mrs. McWaid gave Patrick another hug.

"Did you see that crowbar shoot out of the roof, Patrick?"

Michael pointed at a spot in the river. "Just like a cannon. Did you do that?"

Patrick nodded, and he finally understood what had happened.

"I guess the steam shot it out of there," he whispered weakly. "After I hit it loose."

"Patrick." Mrs. McWaid held her son's face in her hands. "I can't believe you're in the middle of all this."

"Well . . ."

"We had no idea where you were," she added, "and the magistrate wouldn't even let us off the boat to look."

"We tried, though," added Becky.

"Jasper *did* tell us what happened with Mr. Li," Mrs. McWaid continued between her tears. She held her son at arm's length. "But we had no idea what happened to you or why . . ."

Patrick opened his mouth, then closed it. His head still hurt. How could he explain it all?

"This trouble," said Jasper, shaking her head. "It was all my fault, not Patrick's. He was only trying to help me."

"Would you please stop saying everything is your fault?" Patrick scolded her halfheartedly. "It's not your fault. You have no idea. I don't know how you can say that."

"I should have come back sooner," she replied. "But I was scared. I wanted to go to my father, but—"

"But she came back here to the *Lady E*!" put in Michael. He set Christopher down on the deck.

"And *you're* not well, Patrick." Mrs. McWaid took a closer look at her son. "John, look at him. He's weak and has lost his voice, and he's shaking, the same way Jasper was!"

Mr. McWaid ducked out of the engine room, where steam still filled the air.

"Are you sick?" asked Michael, looking curiously at his older brother.

"It was worse a few days ago."

"Every time we let you out of our sight," said Mrs. McWaid, "you come home with some kind of horrible injury."

Patrick still didn't know how to explain everything that had happened to him in the past three days. He wasn't sure himself what had happened exactly, so he just sat down, still shaking. "I think maybe it's because I drank bad water from the ship. . . ."

"If it *is* typhoid," said Mr. McWaid, feeling Patrick's forehead, "you're going to get over it, the same as Jasper. But we're going to put you in bed under lock and key, if that's what it takes."

That didn't sound so bad. Patrick searched the wharf for signs of Mr. Li and the others. Only a couple of men in uniform showed up.

"I'm really sorry it turned out this way." Patrick rolled over on his bed the next morning and stared up at his visitor. This time it had been Patrick's turn to sleep in the captain's cabin. He could hear Sunday morning church bells in the distance.

"What are you sorry about?" wondered Jasper. "The quarantine is over, except for you being stuck in this room for the next couple of weeks. Mr. Gipps and his friends are in jail. You can load your cargo now and go back up the river."

"I was thinking you might be able to come with us."

"Thanks. But I have been enough trouble." Jasper shook her head. "And you know I have to go find my father. And Mr. Li . . ."

"Still out there, I know."

Jasper nodded. "Mr. Li might still cause trouble for the Chinese people in Ballarat. Since all the other men are going now, I have to go, too."

"At least ride with us up the river for a few miles," Patrick suggested, trying to lean on his elbow. "We can get you closer on the river. You won't have to walk as far."

Jasper smiled. "Are you saying girls cannot walk as far as boys?"

"No. I'm just saying it would be fun to have you on the *Lady E*. I mean, I went to all the trouble of hiding you and getting sick and carrying your father's statue. . . ."

His voice trailed off. *The statue.*

"It is all right." Jasper bit her lip and her voice quivered just a bit. "I know you did not mean to lose it. You did your best."

"Lose it?" Patrick couldn't believe he had forgotten about the statue. But after all the excitement, Jasper hadn't said anything. "I didn't lose it!" He began to sit up.

"Patrick, you are not supposed to get up."

Patrick waved her off. "Under the wharf. Meet me there in five minutes."

It was simple, really. Patrick just retraced his steps to the place where he had been hiding with Wilberforce the night before. He made a wide turn around Wilberforce, though. The donkey was waiting patiently on the wharf, where someone had tied him to a piling.

From there Patrick slipped around the side and down the plank to the mud and rocks under the wharf.

I'll be back in bed in a minute.

"What are you doing down there?" Jasper peered through the cracks from above, down into the shadows.

"Here it is," he told her. He reached down to pluck the familiar shape of the bag out of the mud.

"You are not making any sense at all."

"Perfect sense. See?" He reached proudly into the bag to hold up the ivory koala statue in the light that filtered down from above. But the mud on his hands was more slippery than he'd thought.

"Patrick, be careful!"

Patrick watched in horror as the statue slipped from his grip and flew through the air to hit a large, sharp-edged rock with a sickening *crack!*

"Oh no." Patrick groaned. Jasper flew down the plank and was there to pick up the statue herself.

"I'm so sorry, Jasper." Patrick reached out to take the treasure, but his hands were still muddy. "It was an accident. Now I've ruined everything for you."

Jasper just picked up the three pieces of the statue. She didn't say anything, but Patrick knew it was ruined. He knew how he would have felt.

"After all this," moaned Patrick. "It would have been better to have left it there. I should have stayed in bed."

"No, look." Jasper began to smile from ear to ear. She walked slowly out into the sunshine and held up the pieces to the light. "Look at this, Patrick."

Patrick noticed a dull glitter between the pieces of the koala. He looked closer to see a good-sized nugget carefully notched into the hollow of the statue. It was so carefully hidden, they had never noticed a seam. Patrick couldn't stop staring.

"That's the biggest gold nugget I've ever seen, Jasper." Patrick felt a tingle up his spine. They had just discovered a treasure.

"So this is what my father really sent us," Jasper finally whispered. "For passage to Australia. My mother would have known."

Patrick nodded. He guessed the nugget was surely worth a small fortune. Enough to have brought Jasper and her family to Australia, and much more. Enough now to buy Jasper's freedom from Mr. Li. And though it seemed like such a serious moment, the only thing Patrick could do was giggle. Jasper didn't seem to mind.

"I was never worried about how things would turn out," Patrick told her as she turned the nugget around and around in the sun. "Didn't I tell you everything was going to be all right?"

"As I recall, it was *me* telling *you*."

"Oh no." Patrick was ready to tease. "It was me. I remember distinctly saying, 'Jasper, don't you worry, God is going to take care of you—' "

Patrick heard a scratching noise above their heads and jumped.

But it was only a crow that had landed to inspect a leftover clam meal on the edge of the wharf. Another crow joined him, and they squabbled beak-to-beak with their loud *ark-ark-ark* calls. Wilberforce joined in with a *hee-haw* of his own.

Jasper laughed. "Just like He takes care of the raven, right?"

"Right. That and the donkey, too."

THE CHINESE IN AUSTRALIA, 1869

Koala Beach Outbreak takes Patrick McWaid and his family dangerously close to a challenging chapter in Australia's history: the arrival of Chinese miners eager to make their fortunes in the goldfields. Thousands came after gold was first discovered near Bathurst in New South Wales in 1851. A large number—just like Jasper—came from the Guangdong Province, especially from the great city of Canton. In Australia, Robe really was a landing point.

They came by ship, of course, and in this adventure the shipwreck scene is based on recorded historic fact. Several shipwrecks actually did occur near the mouth of the Murray River, though most of the dangerous rock outcroppings were actually a few miles farther south. It is also possible that some of the immigrant miners could have been Christians, since the first Protestant missionary to China, Robert Morrison, landed in Canton in 1807.

But there was a problem.

Just as in the young United States, a few people already living in Australia struggled with what they thought was a Chinese "threat." Often the Chinese miners were content to work mining claims that no one else wanted. Most of them worked very hard.

So a handful of European-Australian miners resented the Chinese immigrants. Several riots and clashes are recorded in history books, particularly when Chinese workers were brought in to replace striking miners. In some cases, entire Chinese communities in the mining regions were destroyed. Their language, customs, and religion were very different and hard for the Europeans to understand.

Part of the "threat" may also have been confused with a fear of dangerous epidemics. Epidemics of typhoid and influenza did threaten the health of many people during those years—not just in China and Australia, but all over the world. Life was risky without the drugs and modern medical treatments we take for granted today. What's more, people often didn't understand how the diseases were spread. (Remember all the different ideas people had in the book? "Vapors"?) When people didn't understand, it was easy to blame.

That's the darker side of history, a part of the past we'd like to forget. Even though it's much better today, we cannot forget—not if we want to make sure it doesn't happen that way again. And by remembering, we discover the good news: There are a lot of stories with happy endings, too. Stories of brave Australians like Patrick and Becky. People with the courage to live what they believed. People with the spirit to make a difference.

Australian Christians, in fact, were some of the first to establish good schools and fair newspapers in their country. They were doctors, paddle-steamer captains, and pastors. Mothers and fathers. Bricklayers. Laborers. And, of course, kids.

These people had at least one thing in common. Because of their faith, they wanted to reach out and put their beliefs into action. They wanted to make a difference in their new country. And they knew they would have to look past the color of a person's skin or the shape of their eyes to discover the needs on the inside.

No one said it would be easy. After all, Australians came from so many different places. But it's still worth the effort today, just as it was in 1869.

Be sure to read Book 8 in the exciting
ADVENTURES DOWN UNDER!
Panic at Emu Flat

"What's it feel like to be fourteen?" asks Michael. "Not much different" is Patrick's reply. But growing up is a problem aboard the McWaid family's paddle steamer. There's the boatload of ostriches. There's Mr. McWaid's job offer back in Ireland. There's the Bible-quoting Miss Perlmutter, with her dozens of mysterious barrels. And then there's Jeff, Patrick's good friend, acting distant and afraid. But after a late-night run-in with a dangerous bully, Patrick's problems have only just begun! Determined to uncover Jeff's secret and to clear his own name, Patrick's quest ultimately leads to a hair-raising chase through the corridors of Collingwood Asylum!

A note from the author . . .

One of the best parts about writing is hearing back from readers—so please feel free to ask me a question or just let me know what you thought of this adventure. And check out some of the other books in ADVENTURES DOWN UNDER as well as the exciting World War II adventures in THE YOUNG UNDERGROUND! You can drop me a line, care of Bethany House Publishers, 11400 Hampshire Avenue South, Minneapolis, Minnesota, 55438. I'll look forward to hearing from you!

P.S. Now you can visit me online at www.coolreading.com!

Series for Middle Graders* From BHP

ADVENTURES DOWN UNDER · by Robert Elmer
When Patrick McWaid's father is unjustly sent to Australia as a prisoner in 1867, the rest of the family follows, uncovering action-packed mystery along the way.

ADVENTURES OF THE NORTHWOODS · by Lois Walfrid Johnson
Kate O'Connell and her stepbrother Anders encounter mystery and adventure in northwest Wisconsin near the turn of the century.

AN AMERICAN ADVENTURE SERIES · by Lee Roddy
Hildy Corrigan and her family must overcome danger and hardship during the Great Depression as they search for a "forever home."

BLOODHOUNDS, INC. · by Bill Myers
Hilarious, hair-raising suspense follows brother-and-sister detectives Sean and Melissa Hunter in these madcap mysteries with a message.

GIRLS ONLY! · by Beverly Lewis
Four talented young athletes become fast friends as together they pursue their Olympic dreams.

JOURNEYS TO FAYRAH · by Bill Myers
Join Denise, Nathan, and Josh on amazing journeys as they discover the wonders and lessons of the mystical Kingdom of Fayrah.

MANDIE BOOKS · by Lois Gladys Leppard
With over four million sold, the turn-of-the-century adventures of Mandie and her many friends will keep readers eager for more.

THE RIVERBOAT ADVENTURES · by Lois Walfrid Johnson
Libby Norstad and her friend Caleb face the challenges and risks of working with the Underground Railroad during the mid–1800s.

TRAILBLAZER BOOKS · by Dave and Neta Jackson
Follow the exciting lives of real-life Christian heroes through the eyes of child characters as they share their faith with others around the world.

THE TWELVE CANDLES CLUB · by Elaine L. Schulte
When four twelve-year-old girls set up a business of odd jobs and baby-sitting, they uncover wacky adventures and hilarious surprises.

THE YOUNG UNDERGROUND · by Robert Elmer
Peter and Elise Andersen's plots to protect their friends and themselves from Nazi soldiers in World War II Denmark guarantee fast-paced action and suspenseful reads.

*(ages 8–13)

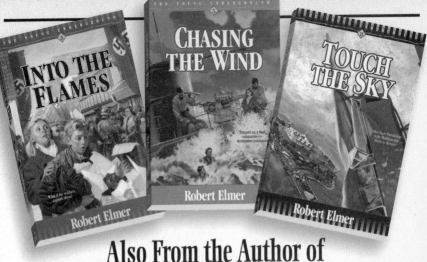

Also From the Author of
THE ADVENTURES DOWN UNDER!

Boys and girls from all over the country write to Robert Elmer telling him how much they love THE YOUNG UNDERGROUND books—have you read them?

In THE YOUNG UNDERGROUND, eleven-year-old Peter Andersen and his twin sister, Elise, are living in the city of Helsingor, Denmark, during World War II. There are German soldiers everywhere—on the streets, in patrol boats in the harbor, and in fighter planes in the sky. Peter and Elise must help their Jewish friend Henrik and his parents escape to Sweden. But with Nazi boats patrolling the sea, they'll need a miracle to get their friends to safety!

Throughout the series Peter and Elise come face-to-face with guard dogs, arsonists, and spies. Together they rescue a downed British bomber pilot, search for treasure, become trapped on a Nazi submarine, and uncover a plot to assassinate the King of Denmark!

Read all eight exciting, danger-filled books in THE YOUNG UNDERGROUND!

A Way Through the Sea   *Chasing the Wind*

Beyond the River   *A Light in the Castle*

Into the Flames   *Follow the Star*

Far From the Storm   *Touch the Sky*

Available from your local Christian bookstores or from Bethany House Publishers.

The Leader in Christian Fiction!

BETHANY HOUSE PUBLISHERS

11400 Hampshire Ave. South
Minneapolis, MN 55438

www.bethanyhouse.com